Winters Tales 24

Winter's Tales

24

EDITED BY

A. D. Maclean

ST. MARTIN'S
NEW YORK

St. Martin's Press, Inc., 175 Fifth Ave., New York, N.Y. 10010

Printed in Great Britain

Library of Congress Catalog Card Number: 78–62763

First published in the United States of America in 1979

ISBN 0–312–88412–5

Contents

Acknowledgements

Shirley Hazzard's 'A Crush on Doctor Dance' has been published in *The New Yorker*, Nicholas Hasluck's 'The Hat on the Letter "O"' has been published by the Fremantle Arts Centre, Australia.

Editor's Note

THIS YEAR's collection contains stories by four writers whose work I'm ashamed to say I had not previously known. However, better late. David Paul recently published in America a trilogy of his translations of the poetry and prose of Rimbaud, Baudelaire and Mallarmé and has just completed a novella. Diana Petre is the author of *The Secret Orchard of Roger Ackerley* (Hamish Hamilton) and is writing the biography of Lady Reading. Nicholas Hasluck's first novel, *Quarantine*, was published this year and a collection of his stories is due next year. Thomas M. Disch is publishing a novel, *On the Wings of Song* (Gollancz), this autumn and is at work on another.

The other contributors will be known to most readers for their stories and/or their novels and I shall only say that the 'mix' seems to me to be a good one and that I hope that you enjoy it.

A.D.M.

The Man Who Had No Idea

THOMAS M. DISCH

AT FIRST he'd assumed that he'd failed. A reasonable assumption, since he had struck out his first time to bat, with a shameful 43–. But when two weeks had gone by and there was still no word from the Board of Examiners he wondered if maybe he'd managed to squeak through. He didn't see how he could have. The examiner, a wizened white-haired fuddy-duddy whose name Barry instantly forgot, had been hostile and aggressive right from the word go, telling Barry that he thought his handshake was too sincere. He directed the conversation first to the possible dangers of excessive sunbathing, which was surely an oblique criticism of Barry's end-of-August tan and the leisure such a tan implied, then started in on the likelihood that dolphins were as intelligent as people. Barry, having entered the cubicle resolved to stake all his chips on a tactic of complete candour, had said, one, he was too young to worry about skin cancer and, two, he had no interest in animals except as meat. This started the examiner off on the psychic experiences of some woman he'd read about in *Reader's Digest*. Barry couldn't get a toehold anywhere on the smooth façade of the man's compulsive natter. He got the feeling, more and more, that *he* was keeping score and the old fart was being tested, an attitude that did not bode well. Finally, with ten minutes left on the clock, he'd just upped and left, which was not, strictly speaking, a violation. It did imply that some kind of closure had been achieved, which definitely was not the case; he'd panicked, pure and simple. A fiasco from which he'd naturally feared the worst in the form of a letter addressed to Dear Applicant. ('We regret to inform you, etc....') But possibly the old fart had been making things deliberately difficult, testing him; possibly his reactions hadn't been that entirely inappropriate. Possibly he'd passed.

When another two weeks went by without the Board of Examiners saying boo, he couldn't stand the suspense any longer and went down to Center Street to fill out a form that asked basically where did he stand. A clerk coded the form and fed it into the computer. The computer instructed Barry to fill out another form, giving more details. Fortunately he'd brought the data the computer wanted, so he was able to fill out the second form on the spot. After a wait of less than ten minutes his number lighted up on the board and he was told to go to Window 28.

Window 28 was the window that issued licences: he had passed!

'I passed,' he announced incredulously to the clerk at the window.

The clerk had the licence with his name on it, Barry Riordan, right there in her hand. She inserted it into the slot of a grey machine, which responded with an authoritative *chunk*. She slid the validated licence under the grille.

'Do you know, I still can't believe it. This is *my* licence. That's really incredible.'

The clerk tapped the shut-up button pinned on the neckband of her tee-shirt.

'Oh. Sorry. I didn't notice. Well ... thanks.'

He smiled at her, a commiserating guilty smile, and she smiled back, a mechanical next-please smile.

He didn't look at the licence till he was out in the street. Stapled to the back of it was a printed notice:

IMPORTANT

Owing to the recent systems overload error your test results of 24 August have been erased. Therefore, in accordance with Bylaw 9(*c*), Section XII, of the Revised Federal Communications Act, you are being issued a Temporary Licence, valid for three months from the date of issue, subject to the restrictions set forth in Appendix II of the Federal Communications Handbook (18th edition).

You may re-apply for another examination at any time. An examination score in or above the eighth percentile will secure the removal of all restrictions and you will immediately receive your Permanent Licence. A score in the sixth or seventh percentiles will not affect the validity of your Temporary Licence, though its expiration date may be extended by this means for a period of up to three months. A score in the fifth percentile or below will result in the withdrawal of your Temporary Licence.

Holders of a Temporary Licence are advised to study Chapter Nine ('The Temporary Licence') in the Federal Communications Handbook. Remember that direct interactive personal communications are one of our most valuable heritages. Use your licence wisely. Do not abuse the privilege of free speech.

So, in fact, he hadn't passed the exam. Or maybe he had. He'd never find out.

His first elation fizzled out and he was left with his usual flattened sense of personal inconsequence. Tucking the licence into his ID folder, he felt like a complete charlatan, a nobody pretending to be a somebody. If he'd scored in the first percentile, he'd have been issued this licence the same as if he'd scored in the tenth. And he knew with *a priori* certainty that he hadn't done that well. The most he'd hoped for was another seven points, just enough to tip him over the edge, into the sixth percentile. Instead he'd had dumb luck.

Not to worry, he advised himself. The worst is over. You've got your licence. How you got it doesn't matter.

Oh, yeah, another and less friendly inward voice replied. Now all you need are three endorsements. Lots of luck.

Well, I'll *get* them, he insisted, hoping to impress the other voice with the authenticity and vitality of his self-confidence. But the other voice wasn't impressed, and so, instead of going straight from Center Street to the nearest speakeasy to celebrate, he took the subway home and spent the evening watching first a fascinating documentary on calcium structures and then 'Celebrity Circus', with Willy Marx. Willy had four guests: a famous prostitute, a tax accountant who had just published his memoirs, a comedian who did a surrealistic skit about a speakeasy for five-year-olds, and a novelist with a speech impediment who got into an argument with the comedian about whether his skit was essentially truthful or unjustifiably cruel. In the middle of their argument Barry came down with a murderous headache, took two aspirins, and went to bed. Just before he fell asleep, he thought: I could call them and tell them what *I* thought.

But what did he think?

He didn't know.

That, in a nutshell, was Barry's problem. At last he had his licence and could talk to anyone he wanted to talk to, but he didn't know what to talk *about*. He had no ideas of his own. He agreed with anything anyone said. The skit had been *both* essentially truthful *and* unjustifiably cruel. Too much sunbathing probably *was* dangerous. Porpoises probably *were* as smart as people.

Fortunately for his morale, this state of funk did not continue long. Barry didn't let it. The next night he was off to Partyland, a 23rd Street speakeasy that advertised heavily on late-night TV. As he approached the froth of electric lights cantilevered over the entrance, Barry could feel the middle of his body turning hollow with excitement, his throat and tongue getting tingly.

There was only a short line, and in a moment he was standing in front of the box-office window. 'Ring?' the window asked. He looked at the price-list. 'Second,' he said, and slid his Master-Charge into the appropriate slot. 'Licence, please,' said the window, winking an arrow that pointed at another slot. He inserted his licence into the other slot, a bell went ding, and *mira*! he was inside Partyland, ascending the big blue escalator up to his first first-hand experience of direct interactive personal communication. Not a classroom exercise, not a therapy session, not a job briefing, not an ecumenical agape, but an honest-to-God conversation, spontaneous, unstructured, and all his own.

The usher who led him to his seat in the second ring sat down beside him and started to tell him about a Japanese department store that covered an entire sixteen and a half acres, had thirty-two restaurants, two movie theatres, and a children's playground.

'That's fascinating, isn't it?' the usher concluded, after setting forth further facts about this remarkable department store.

'I suppose it is,' Barry said non-committally. He couldn't figure out why the usher wanted to tell him about a department store in Japan.

'I forget where I read about it,' the usher said. 'In some magazine or other. Well, mix in, enjoy yourself, and if you want to order anything there's a console that rolls out from this end table.' He demonstrated.

The usher continued to hover, smiling, over his chair. Finally Barry realised he was waiting for a tip. Without any idea of what was customary, he gave him a dollar, which seemed to do the trick.

He sat there in his bulgy sponge of a chair, grateful to be alone and able to take in the sheer size and glamour of the place. Partyland was an endless middle-class living-room, a panorama of all that was gracious, tasteful and posh. At least from here in the second ring it *seemed* endless. It had a seating capacity, according to its ads, of 780, but tonight wasn't one of its big nights and a lot of the seats were empty.

At intervals that varied unpredictably the furniture within this living-room would re-arrange itself, and suddenly you would find yourself face to face with a new conversational partner. You could also, for a few dollars more, hire a sofa or armchair that you could drive at liberty among the other chairs, choosing your partners rather than leaving them to chance. Relatively few patrons of Partyland exercised this option, since the whole point of the place was that you could just sit back and let your chair do the driving.

The background music changed from Vivaldi's 'Four Seasons' to a Sondheim medley, and all the chairs in Barry's area suddenly lifted their occupants up in the air and carried them off, legs dangling, to their next conversational destination. Barry found himself sitting next to a girl in a red velvet evening dress with a hat of paper feathers and polyhedrons. The band of the hat said, 'I'm a Partyland Smarty-pants.'

'Hi,' said the girl in a tone intended to convey a worldly-wise satiety but that achieved no more than blank anomie. 'What's up?'

'Terrific, just terrific,' Barry replied with authentic warmth. He'd always scored well at this preliminary stage of basic communication, which was why, at the time, he'd so much resented his examiner's remark about his handshake. There was nothing phoney about his handshake, and he knew it.

'I like your shoes,' she said.

Barry looked down at his shoes. 'Thanks.'

'I like shoes pretty much generally,' she went on. 'I guess you could say I'm a kind of shoe freak.' She snickered wanly.

Barry smiled, at a loss.

'But yours are particularly nice. How much did you pay for them, if you don't mind my asking?'

Though he minded, he hadn't the gumption to say so. 'I don't remember. Not a lot. They're really nothing special.'

'*I* like them,' she insisted. Then, 'My name's Cinderella. What's yours?'

'Is it really?'

'Really. You want to see my ID?'

'Mm.'

She dug into her ID folder, which was made of the same velvet as her dress, and took out her licence. It was blue, like his (a Temporary Licence), and, again like his, there was a staple in the upper left-hand corner.

'See?' she said. 'Cinderella B. Johnson. It was my mother's idea. My mother has a really weird sense of humour sometimes. She's dead now, though. Do you like it?'

'Like what?'

'My name.'

'Oh, yeah, sure.'

'Because some people don't. They think it's affected. But I can't help the name I was born with, can I?'

'I was going to ask you—'

Her face took on the intent yet mesmerised look of a quiz-show contestant. 'Ask, ask.'

'The staple on your licence – why is it there?'

'What staple?' she countered, becoming in an instant rigid with suspicion, like a hare that scents a predator.

'The one on your licence. Was there something attached to it originally?'

'Some notice ... I don't know. How can I remember

something like that? Why do you ask?'

'There's one like it on mine.'

'So? If you ask me, this is a damned stupid topic for a conversation. Aren't you going to tell me *your* name?'

'Uh ... Rex.'

'Rex what?'

'Rex Riordan.'

'An Irish name. That explains it, then.'

He looked at her questioningly.

'That must be where you got your gift of the gab. You must have kissed the Blarney stone.'

She's crazy, he thought.

But crazy in a dull, not an interesting way. He wondered how long they'd have to go on talking before the chairs switched round again. It seemed such a waste of time talking to another temp, since he could only get the endorsements he needed from people who held Permanent Licences. Of course, the practice was probably good for him. You can't expect to like everyone you meet, as the Communications Handbook never tired of pointing out, but you can always try to make a good impression. Someday you'd meet someone it was crucial to hit it off with and your practice would pay off.

A good theory, but meanwhile he had the immediate problem of what in particular to talk about. 'Have you heard about the giant department store in Japan?' he asked her. 'It covers sixteen acres.'

'Sixteen and a half,' she corrected. 'You must read *Topic*, too.'

'Mm.'

'It's a fascinating magazine. I look at it almost every week. Sometimes I'm just too busy, but usually I skim it, at least.'

'Busy doing ...?'

'Exactly.' She squinted across the vast tasteful expanse of Partyland, then stood up and waved. 'I think I've *recognised* someone,' she said excitedly, preening her paper feathers with her free hand. Far away someone waved back.

Cinderella broke one of the polyhedrons off her hat and put it on her chair. 'So I'll remember which it is,' she explained. Then, contritely, 'I hope you don't mind.'

'Not at all.'

Left to himself he couldn't stop thinking about the staple he'd seen on her licence. It was like the seemingly insignificant clue in a detective story from which the solution to the whole mystery gradually unfolds. For didn't it strongly suggest that she, too, had been given the benefit of the doubt, that she'd got her licence not because her score entitled her to it but thanks to Bylaw 9(*c*), Section XII? The chagrin of being classified in the same category as such a nitwit! Partyland was probably *full* of people in their situation, all hoping to connect with some bona fide Permanent Licence-holder, instead of which they went around colliding with each other.

A highly depressing idea, but he did not on that account roll out the console to select a remedy from the menu. He knew from long experience that whatever could make him palpably happier was also liable to send him into a state of fugue in which conversation in the linear sense became next to impossible. So he passed the time till the next switchover by working out, in his head, the square roots of various five-digit numbers. Then, when he had a solution, he'd check it on his calculator. He'd got five right answers when his chair reared up, God bless it, and bore him off towards.... Would it be the couple chained, wrist to wrist, on the blue settee? No, at the last moment, his chair veered left and settled down in front of an unoccupied bentwood rocker. A sign in the seat of the rocker said, 'I feel a little sick. Back in five minutes.'

Barry was just getting used to the idea of going on to six-digit figures when a woman in a green sofa wheeled up to him and asked what kind of music he liked.

'Any kind, really.'

'Any or none, it amounts to much the same thing.'

'No, honestly. Whatever is playing, I usually like it. What are they playing here? I like that.'

'Muzak,' she said dismissively.

It was, in fact, still the Sondheim medley, but he let that pass. It wasn't worth an argument.

'What do you do?' she demanded.

'I simulate a job that Citibank is developing for another corporation, but only on an auxiliary basis. Next year I'm supposed to start full-time.'

She grimaced. 'You're new at Partyland, aren't you?'

He nodded. 'First time tonight. In fact, this is my first time ever in any speakeasy. I just got my licence yesterday.'

'Well, welcome to the club.' With a smile that might as well have been a sneer. 'I suppose you're looking for endorsements?'

Not from you, he wanted to tell her. Instead he looked off into the distance at the perambulations of a suite of chairs in another ring. Only when all the chairs had settled into place did he refocus on the woman in the foreground. He realised with a little zing of elation that he had just administered his first snub!

'What did Freddy say when you came in?' she asked in a conspiratorial if not downright friendly tone. (His snub had evidently registered.)

'Who is Freddy?'

'The usher who showed you to your seat. I saw him sit down and talk with you.'

'He told me about some Japanese department store.'

She nodded knowingly. 'Of course – I should have known. Freddy shills for *Topic* magazine and that's one of their featured stories this week. I wonder what they pay him. Last week their cover story was about Irina Khokolovna, and all Freddy could talk about was Irina Khokolovna.

'Who is Irina Khokolovna?' he asked.

She hooted a single derisory hoot. 'I thought you said you liked music!'

'I do,' he protested. But, clearly, he had just failed a major test. With a sigh of weariness and a triumphant smile, the woman rotated her sofa one hundred and eighty degrees and drove off in the direction of the couple chained together on the blue settee.

The couple rose in unison and greeted her with cries of 'Maggie!' and 'Son of a gun!' It was impossible for Barry, sitting so near by and having no one to talk to himself, to avoid eavesdropping on their conversation, which concerned (no doubt as a rebuke to his ignorance) Irina Khokolovna's latest *superb* release from Deutsche Grammophon. She was at her best in Schumann, but her Wolf was *comme ci, comme ça*. Even so, Khokolovna's Wolf was miles ahead of Adriana Motta's, or even Gwyneth Batterham's, who for all her real intelligence was developing a distinct wobble in her upper register. Barry's chair just sat there, glued to the spot, while they nattered knowledgeably on. He wished he were home watching Willy Marx – or anywhere but Partyland.

'Mine's Ed,' said the occupant of the bentwood rocker, a young man of Barry's own age, build, and hair-style.

'Pardon?' said Barry.

'I said,' he said, with woozy precision, 'my name is Ed.'

'Oh. Mine's Barry. How are you, Ed?'

He held out his hand. Ed shook it gravely.

'You know, Barry,' Ed said, 'I've been thinking about what you were saying, and I think the whole problem is *cars*. Know what I mean?'

'Elaborate,' Barry suggested.

'Right. The thing about cars is.... Well, I live in Elizabeth, across the river, right? So any time I come here I've got to drive, right? Which you might think was a drag but, in fact, I always feel terrific. You know?'

Barry nodded. He didn't understand what Ed was saying in any very specific way, but he knew he agreed with him.

'I feel...free. If that doesn't seem too ridiculous. Whenever I'm driving my car.'

'What have you got?' Barry asked.

'A Toyota.'

'Nice. Very nice.'

'I don't think I'm unique that way,' said Ed.

'No, I wouldn't say so.'

'Cars *are* freedom. And so what all this talk about an energy crisis boils down to is—' He stopped short. 'I think I'm having a fugue.'

'I think maybe you are. But that's all right. I do, too. It'll pass.'

'Listen, what's your name?'

'Barry,' Barry said. 'Barry Riordan.'

Ed held out his hand. 'Mine's Ed. Say, are you trying to pick up an endorsement?'

Barry nodded. 'You, too?'

'No. In fact, I think I've still got one left. Would you like it?'

'Jesus,' said Barry. 'Yeah, sure.

Ed took out his ID folder, took his licence from the folder, tickled the edge of the endorsement sticker from the back of the licence with his finger-nail, and offered it to Barry.

'You're sure you want me to have this?' Barry asked, incredulous, with the white curlicue of the sticker dangling from his finger-tip.

Ed nodded. 'You remind me of somebody.'

'Well, I'm awfully grateful. Really. I mean, you

scarcely know me.'

'Right,' said Ed, nodding more vigorously. 'But I liked what you were saying about cars. That made a lot of sense.'

'You know,' Barry burst out in a sudden access of confessional bonhomie, 'I feel confused *most* of the time.'

'Right.'

'But I can never express it. Everything I *say* seems to make more sense than what I can feel inside of me.'

'Right, right.'

The music changed from the Sondheim medley to the flip side of 'The Four Seasons', and Barry's chair lifted him up and bore him off towards the couple in the blue settee, while Ed, limp in the bentwood rocker, was carried off in the opposite direction.

'Goodbye,' Barry shouted after him, but Ed was already either comatose or out of earshot. 'And thanks again!'

The MacKinnons introduced themselves. His name was Jason. Hers was Michelle. They lived quite near by, on West 28th, and were interested, primarily, in the television shows they'd seen when they were growing up, about which they were very well informed. Despite a bad first impression, due to his associating them with Maggie of the green sofa, Barry found himself liking the MacKinnons enormously, and before the next switchover he put his chair in the LOCK position. They spent the rest of the evening together, exchanging nostalgic titbits over coffee and slices of Partyland's famous pineapple pie. At closing-time he asked if either of them would consider giving him an endorsement. They said they would have, having thoroughly enjoyed his company, but unfortunately they'd used up their quota for that year. They seemed genuinely sorry, but he felt, even so, that it had been a mistake to ask.

*

His first endorsement proved to have been beginner's luck. Though he went almost every night to a different speakeasy and practically lived at Partyland during the weekends, when it was at its liveliest, he never again had such a plum fall in his lap. He didn't get within sniffing distance of his heart's desire. Most people he met were temps, and the few Permanent Licence-holders inclined to be friendly to him invariably turned out, like the MacKinnons, to have already disposed of their allotted endorsements. Or so they said. As the weeks went by and anxiety mounted, he began to be of the cynical but widely held opinion that many people simply removed the stickers from their licences so it would *seem* they'd been used. According to Jason MacKinnon, a completely selfless endorsement, like his from Ed, was a rare phenomenon. Quid pro quos were the general rule, in the form either of cash on the barrel for services rendered. Barry said (jokingly, of course) that he wouldn't object to bartering his virtue for an endorsement, or preferably two, to which Michelle replied (quite seriously) that unfortunately she did not know anyone who might be in the market for Barry's particular type. Generally, she observed, it was *younger* people who got their endorsements by putting out.

Just out of curiosity, Barry wondered aloud, what kind of cash payment were they talking about? Jason said the standard fee, a year ago, for a single sticker had been a thousand dollars; two and half for a pair, since people with two blanks to fill could be presumed to be that much more desperate. Owing, however, to a recent disproportion between supply and demand the going price for a single was now seventeen hundred, a double a round four thousand. Jason said he could arrange an introduction at that price, if Barry were interested.

'I will tell you', said Barry, 'what you can do with your stickers.'

'Oh, now,' said Michelle placatingly. 'We're still your *friends*, Mr Riordan, but business is business. If it were our own *personal* stickers we were discussing, we wouldn't *hesitate* to give you an endorsement absolutely *gratis*. Would we, Jason?'

'Of course not, no question.'

'But we're middlemen, you see. We have only limited flexibility in the terms we can offer. Say, fifteen hundred.'

'And three and a half for the pair,' Jason added. 'And that is a rock-bottom offer. You won't do better anywhere else.'

'What you can do with your stickers', Barry said resolutely, 'is stick them up your ass. Your asses, rather.'

'I wish you wouldn't take that attitude, Mr Riordan,' said Jason in a tone of sincere regret. 'We do like you, and we have enjoyed your company. If we didn't, we would certainly not be offering this opportunity.'

'Bullshit,' said Barry. It was the first time he'd used an obscenity conversationally, and he brought it off with great conviction. 'You knew when my licence would expire, and you've just been stringing me along, hoping I'd get panicky.'

'We have been *trying*', said Michelle, 'to help.'

'Thanks. I'll help myself.'

'How?'

'Tomorrow I'm going back to Center Street and take the exam again.'

Michelle MacKinnon leaned across the coffee-table that separated the blue settee from Barry's armchair and gave him a sound motherly smack on the cheek. 'Wonderful! That's the way to meet a challenge – head on! You're bound to pass. After all, you've had three months of practice. You've become much more fluent these past three months.'

'Thanks.' He got up to go.

'Hey!' Jason grabbed Barry's hand and gave it an earnest squeeze. 'Don't forget, if you *do* get your

Permanent Licence—'

'When he gets it,' Michelle amended.

'Right. *When* you get it, you know where you can find us. We're always here on the same settee.'

'You two are unbelievable,' Barry said. 'Do you honestly think I'd sell you my endorsements? Assuming' – he knocked on the varnished walnut coffee-table – 'I pass my exam.'

'It is safer', Michelle said, 'to work through a professional introduction service than to try to peddle them on your own. Even though everyone breaks it, the law is still the law. Individuals operating on their own are liable to get caught, since they don't have an arrangement with the authorities. We do. That's why, for instance, it would do you no good to report us to the Communications Control Office. Others have done so in the past, and it did *them* no good.'

'None of them ever got a Permanent Licence, either,' Jason added, with a twinkle of menace.

'That, I'm sure, was just coincidence,' said Michelle. 'After all, we're speaking of only two cases, and neither of the individuals in question was particularly bright. Bright people wouldn't be so quixotic, would they?' She underlined her question with a Mona Lisa smile, and Barry, for all his indignation and outrage, couldn't keep from smiling back. Anyone who could drop a word like 'quixotic' into the normal flow of conversation and make it seem so natural couldn't be all wrong.

'Don't worry,' he promised, tugging his hand out of Jason's. 'I'm not the quixotic type.'

But, when he said it, it sounded false. It wasn't fair.

Barry was as good as his word and went to Center Street the very next morning to take his third exam. The computer assigned him to Marvin Kolodny, PhD, in Cubicle 183. The initials worried him. He could have coped, this time, with the old fuddy-duddy he'd had last August, but a PhD? It seemed as though they were raising the hurdles each time he came around the track. But his worries evaporated the moment he was in the cubicle and saw that Marvin Kolodny was a completely average young man of twenty-four. His averageness was even a bit unsteady, as though he had to think about it; but, then, most twenty-four-year-olds are self-conscious in just that way.

It's always a shock the first time you come up against some particular kind of authority figure – a dentist, a psychiatrist, a cop – who is younger than you are, but it needn't lead to disaster as long as you let the authority figure know right from the start that you intend to be deferential, and this was a quality that Barry conveyed without trying.

'Hi,' said Barry, with masterful deference. 'I'm Barry Riordan.' Marvin Kolodny responded with a boyish grin and offered his hand. An American flag had been tattooed on his right forearm. On a scroll circling the flagpole was the following inscription:

Let's all
Overthrow
the United States
Government
by Force &
Violence

On his other forearm there was a crudely executed rose with his name underneath: Marvin Kolodny, PhD.

'Do you mean it?' Barry asked, marvelling over Marvin's tattoo as they shook hands. He managed to ask the question without in the least seeming to challenge Marvin Kolodny's authority.

'If I didn't mean it,' said Marvin Kolodny, 'do you think I'd have it tattooed on my arm?'

'I suppose not. It's just so ... unusual.'

'I'm an unusual person,' said Marvin Kolodny,

leaning back in his swivel chair and taking a large pipe from the rack on his desk.

'But doesn't *that* idea' – Barry nodded at the tattoo – 'conflict with your having this particular job? Aren't you part of the US Government yourself?'

'Only for the time being. I'm not suggesting that we overthrow the Government *tomorrow*. A successful revolution isn't possible until the proletariat becomes conscious of their oppression and they can't become conscious of anything until they are as articulate as their oppressors. Language and consciousness aren't independent processes, after all. Talking is thinking turned inside out. No more, no less.'

'And which am I?'

'How's that?'

'Am I a proletarian or an oppressor?'

'Like most of us these days, I would say you're probably a little of each. Are you married, uh ...' (he peeked into Barry's file) '... Barry?'

Barry nodded.

'Then that's one form of oppression right there. Children?'

Barry shook his head.

'Do you live with your wife?'

'Not lately. And even when we were together we never talked to each other, except to say practical things like "When is your programme going to be over?" Some people just aren't that interested in talking. Debra certainly isn't. That's why' – he couldn't resist the chance to explain his earlier failures – 'I did so poorly on my earlier exams. Assuming I *did* get a low score last time, which isn't certain since the results were erased. But, assuming that I did, that's the reason. I never got any practice. The basic day-to-day conversational experiences most people have with their spouses never happened in my case.'

Marvin Kolodny frowned – an ingratiating boyish frown. 'Are you sure you're being entirely honest with yourself, Barry? Few people are completely unwilling to talk about something. We've all got hobbyhorses. What was your wife interested in? Couldn't you have talked about that?'

'In religion, mostly. But she didn't care to talk about it, unless you agreed with her.'

'Have you *tried* to agree with her?'

'Well, you see, Dr Kolodny, what she *believes* is that the end of the world is about to happen. Next February. That's where she's gone now – to Arizona, to wait for it. This is the third time she's taken off.'

'Not an easy woman to discourage, by the sound of it.'

'I think she really *wants* the world to end. And also she *does* like Arizona.'

'Have you considered divorce?' Marvin Kolodny asked.

'No, absolutely not. We're still basically in love. After all, most married couples end up not saying much to each other. Isn't that so? Even before Debra got religious, we weren't in the habit of talking to each other. To tell the truth, Dr Kolodny, I've never been much of a talker. I think I was put off it by the compulsory talk we had to do in high school.'

'That's perfectly natural. I hated compulsory talk myself, though I must admit I was good at it. What about your job, Barry? Doesn't that give you opportunities to develop communication skills?'

'I don't communicate with the public directly. Only with simulations, and their responses tend to be pretty stereotyped.'

'Well, there's no doubt that you have a definite communications problem. But I think it's a problem you can lick! I'll tell you what, Barry: officially, I shouldn't tell you this myself, but I'm giving you a score of sixty-five.' He held up his hand to forestall an effusion. 'Now, let me explain how that breaks down. You do very well in most categories – Affect, Awareness of Others, Relevance, Voice Production, et cetera – but where you do fall down is in Notional Content and Originality. There you could do better.'

'Originality has always been my Waterloo,' Barry admitted. 'I just don't seem to be able to come up with my own ideas. I did have one, though, just this morning on my way here, and I was going to try to slip it in while I was taking the exam, only it never seemed quite natural. Have you ever noticed that you never see baby pigeons? All the pigeons you see out on the street are the same size – full-grown. But where do they come from? Where are the little pigeons? Are they hidden somewhere?' He stopped short, feeling ashamed of his idea. Now that it was out in the open it seemed paltry and insignificant, little better than a joke he'd learned by heart, than which there is nothing more calculated to land you in the bottom percentiles.

Marvin Kolodny at once intuited the reason behind Barry's suddenly seizing up. He was in the business, after all, of understanding unspoken meanings and evaluating them precisely. He smiled a sympathetic mature smile.

'Ideas…,' he said, in a slow deliberative manner, as though each word had to be weighed on a scale before it was put into the sentence, '… aren't … things. Ideas – the most authentic ideas – are the natural effortless result of any vital relationship. Ideas are what happen when people connect with each other creatively.'

Barry nodded.

'Do you mind my giving you some honest advice, Barry?'

'Not at all, Dr Kolodny. I'd be grateful.'

'On your G-47 form you say you spend a lot of time at Partyland and similar speakeasies. I realise that's where you did get your first endorsement, but, really, don't you think you're wasting your time in that sort of place? It's a tourist trap!'

'I'm aware of that,' Barry said, smarting under the rebuke.

'You're not going to meet anyone there but temps and various people who are out to fleece temps. With rare exceptions.'

'I know, I know. But I don't know where *else* to go.'

'Why not try this place?' Marvin Kolodny handed Barry a printed card, which read:

INTENSITY FIVE

A New Experience in
Interpersonal Intimacy

5 Barrow Street
New York 10014

Members Only

'I'll certainly try it,' Barry promised. 'But how do I get to be a member?'

'Tell them Marvin sent you.'

And that was all there was to it – he had passed his exam with a score just five points short of the crucial eighth percentile. Which was a tremendous accomplishment but also rather frustrating in a way, since it meant he'd come *that* close to not having to bother scouting out two more endorsements. Still, with another three months in which to continue his quest and an introduction to Intensity Five, Barry had every reason to be optimistic.

'Thank you, Dr Kolodny,' Barry said, lingering in the doorway of the cubicle. 'Thanks terrifically.'

'That's all right, Barry. Just doing my job.'

'You know...I wish....Of course, I know it's not permissible, you being an examiner and all ... but I wish I knew you in a personal way. Truly. You're a very heavy individual.'

'Thank you, Barry. I know you mean that, and I'm flattered. Well, then—' He took his pipe from his mouth and lifted it in a kind of salute. 'So long. And Merry Christmas.'

Barry left the cubicle feeling so transcendent and relaxed that he was five blocks from Center Street before he remembered that he'd neglected to have his licence revalidated at Window 28. As he headed back to the Federal Communications Building his senses seemed to register all the ordinary details of the city's streets with an unnatural hyped clarity: the smell of sauerkraut steaming up from a hot-dog cart, the glint of the noon sun on the mica mixed into the paving-blocks of the sidewalk, the various shapes and colours of the pigeons – the very pigeons, perhaps, that had inspired his so-called idea earlier that day. But it was true, what he'd said. All the pigeons were the same size.

A block south of the Federal Communications Building he looked up, and there strung out under the cornice of the building was the motto, which he had never noticed before, of the Federal Communications Agency:

PLANNED FREEDOM IS THE ROAD
TO LASTING PROGRESS

So simple, so direct, and yet, when you thought about it, almost impossible to understand.

Barrow Street being right in the middle of one of the city's worst slums, Barry had been prepared (he'd thought) for a lesser degree of stateliness and *bon ton* than that achieved by Partyland, but even so the dismal actuality of Intensity Five went beyond anything he could have imagined. A cavernous one-room basement apartment with bare walls, crackly linoleum over a concrete floor, and radiators that hissed and gurgled ominously without generating a great deal of heat. The furniture consisted of metal folding chairs, most of them folded and stacked, a refreshment-stand that sold orange juice and coffee, and a great many free-standing brim-full metal ash-trays. Having already forked out twenty-five dollars upstairs as his membership fee, Barry felt as though he'd been had, but since the outlay was non-refundable he decided to give the place the benefit of his doubt and loiter a while.

He had been loitering, alone and melancholy, for the better part of an hour, eavesdropping to his right on a conversation about somebody's drastic need to develop a more effective persona and to his left on a discussion of the morality of our involvement in Mexico, when a black woman in a white nylon jumpsuit and a very good imitation calf-length mink swept into the room, took a quick survey of those present, and sat down, unbelievably, by him!

Quick as a light-switch he could feel his throat go dry and his face tighten into a smile of rigid insincerity. He blushed, he trembled, he fainted dead away, but only metaphorically.

'I'm Columbine Brown,' she said, as though that offered an explanation.

Did she expect him to recognise her? She was beautiful enough, certainly, to have been someone he ought to recognise, but if he had seen her on TV he didn't remember. In a way she seemed almost *too* beautiful to be a noted personality, since there is usually something a little idiosyncratic about each of them, so they can be told apart. Columbine Brown was beautiful in the manner not of a celebrity but of a *de luxe* (but not customised) sports car.

'I'm Barry Riordan,' he managed to bring out, tardily.

'Let's put our cards on the table, shall we, Mr Riordan? I am a Permanent Card-holder. What are you?'

'A temp.'

'It's fair to assume, then, that you're here to find an endorsement.'

He began to protest. She stopped him with just one omniscient and devastating glance. He nodded.

'Unfortunately, I have used up my quota. However' – she held up a single perfect finger – 'it's almost the New Year. If you're not in a desperate hurry ...?'

'Oh, I've got till March.'

'I'm not promising anything, you understand. Unless we hit it off. If we do, then fine, you have my endorsement. Fair enough?'

'It's a deal.'

'You feel you can trust me?' She lowered her eyes and tried to look wicked and temptress-like, but it was not in the nature of her kind of beauty to do so.

'Anywhere,' he replied. 'Implicitly.'

'Good.' As though of its own volition her coat slipped off her shoulders on to the back of the folding chair. She turned her head sideways and addressed the old woman behind the refreshment-counter. 'Evelyn, how about an orange juice?' She looked at him. He nodded. 'Make it two.'

Then, as though they'd been waiting for these preliminaries to be concluded, tears sprang to her eyes. A tremor of heartfelt emotion coloured her lovely contralto voice as she said, 'Oh, Jesus, what am I going to do? I can't take any more! I am just so ... so goddamned wretched! I'd like to kill myself. No, that isn't true. I'm confused, Larry. But I know one thing – I am an *angry* woman and I'm going to start fighting back!'

It would have been inconsiderate to break in upon such testimony by mentioning that his name was not, in fact, Larry. What difference does one letter make, after all?

'Have you ever been to the Miss America Pageant on 42nd Street?' she asked him, drying her eyes.

'I can't say I have. I always mean to, but you know how it is. It's the same with the Statue of Liberty. It's always there, so you never get around to it.'

'I'm Miss Georgia.'

'No kidding!'

'I have *been* Miss Georgia six nights a week for the last four years, with matinées on Sunday and Tuesday, and do you suppose in all that time that the audience has ever voted for *me* to be Miss America? Ever?'

'*I* would certainly vote for you.'

'Never once,' she went on fiercely, ignoring his supportiveness. 'It's always Miss Massachusetts, or Miss Ohio, who can't do anything but play a damn jew's harp, if you'll excuse my language, or Miss Oregon, who still can't remember the blocking for "Lovely to Look At", which she has been dancing since before *I* graduated from high school. There's no one in the whole damn line-up who hasn't been crowned at least once. Except me.'

'I'm sorry to hear it.'

'I am a *good* singer. I can tap-dance like a house on fire. My balcony scene would break your heart. And I can say objectively that I've got better legs than anyone except, possibly, Miss Wyoming.'

'But you've never been Miss America,' Barry said sympathetically.

'What do you think that *feels* like, here?' She grabbed a handful of white nylon in the general area of her heart.

'I honestly don't know, Miss...' (he'd forgotten her last name) '... Georgia.'

'At Intensity Five I'm just plain Columbine, honey. The same as you're just Larry. And not knowing isn't much of an answer. Here I am exposing myself in front of you, and you come back with "No Opinion". I don't buy that.'

'Well, to be completely candid, Columbine, it's hard for me to imagine your feeling anything but terrific. To be Miss Georgia and have such a lot of talent – isn't that *enough*? I would have thought you'd be very happy.'

Columbine bit her lip, furrowed her brow, and evidenced, in general, a sudden change of heart. 'God, Larry – you're right! I've been kidding myself: the Pageant isn't my problem – it's my excuse. My problem' – her voice dropped, her eyes avoided his – 'is timeless and well known. I fell in love with the wrong man for me. And now it's too late. Would you like to hear a long story, Larry? A long and very unhappy story?'

'Sure. That's what I'm here for, isn't it?'

She smiled a meaningful unblemished smile and gave his hand a quick trusting squeeze. 'You know, Larry, you're an all-right guy.'

Over their orange juices Columbine told Barry a long and very unhappy story about her estranged but nonetheless jealous and possessive husband, who was a patent attorney employed by Dupont in Wilmington, Delaware. Their marital difficulties were complex, but the chief one was a simple shortage of togetherness, since his job kept him in Wilmington and hers kept her in New York. Additionally, her husband's ideal of conversation was very divergent from her own. He enjoyed talking about money, sports and politics with other men, and bottled up all his deeper feelings. She was introspective, outgoing, and warm-hearted.

'It would be all right for a while,' she recalled. 'But the pressure would build until I had to go out and find someone to talk to. It is a basic human need, after all. Perhaps *the* basic need. I had no choice.'

'And then he'd find out, I suppose,' said Barry.

She nodded. 'And go berserk. It was awful. No one can live that way.'

Barry thought that in many ways her problem bore a resemblance to his, at least in so far as they both had to look for intellectual companionship outside the bonds of marriage. But when he began to elaborate upon this insight and draw some interesting parallels between his experience and hers Columbine became impatient. She did not come right out and tell him that he was in breach of contract, but that was definitely the message conveyed by her glazed inattention. Responsive to her needs, he resisted the impulse to make any further contributions of his own and sat back and did his level best to be a good listener and nothing more.

When Columbine had finally run the gamut of all her feelings, which included fear, anger, joy, pain, and an abiding and entirely unreasoning sense of dread, she thanked him, gave him her address and phone number, and said to get in touch in January for his endorsement.

Jubilation, he thought. Bingo. Hallelujah.

But not quite. He still had to get one more endorsement. But now it seemed possible, likely, even inevitable. A matter, merely, of making the effort and reaping the reward.

Dame Fortune had become so well disposed to him that he got his third endorsement (though, in point of hard fact, his second) the very next night. The fated encounter took place at Morone's One-Stop Shopping, a mom-and-pop mini-grocery on 6th Avenue right next to the International Supermarket. Although Morone's charged more for most items, Barry preferred shopping there because it offered such a limited and unchallenging range of choices (cold meats, canned goods, beer, Nabisco cookies) that he never felt intimidated and ashamed of his selections at the check-out counter. He hated to cook, but was that any reason he should be made to feel inadequate? Morone's was made to order for people like Barry, of which there are great numbers.

That night, as he was hesitating between a dinner of Spam and Chef Boy-ar-dee ravioli or Spam and Green Giant corn niblets, the woman who had been standing in front of the frozen-food locker suddenly started talking to herself. The Morones looked at each other in alarm. Neither of them was a licensed talker, which was a further attraction of their store, since one's exchanges with them were limited to such basic permissible amenities as 'How are you?' 'Take care', and giving out prices.

What the woman was saying was of a character to suggest that she had just that minute gone crazy. 'The pain', she explained calmly to the ice-cream section of the freezer, 'only comes on when I do this.' She stooped closer to the ice cream and winced. 'But then it's pure hell. I want to cut my leg off, have a lobotomy, anything to make it stop. Yet I know the problem isn't in my leg at all. It's in my back. Here.' She touched the small of her back. 'A kind of short circuit. Worse than bending over is twisting sideways. Even turning my head can set it off. Sometimes, when I'm alone, I'll start crying just at the thought of it, at knowing I've become so damned superannuated.' She sighed. 'Well, it happens to everyone, and I suppose it could be worse. There's no use complaining. Life goes on, as they say.'

Having come round to a sensible accepting attitude, she turned from the freezer to witness the effect of her outburst on the Morones, who looked elsewhere, and on Barry, who couldn't resist meeting her eyes head-on. Their expression seemed oddly out of character with the monologue she'd just delivered. They were piercing (as against vulnerable) steely-grey eyes that stared defiance from a face all sags and wrinkles. Without the contradiction of such eyes, her face would have seemed ruined and hopeless; with them, she looked just like an ancient centurion in a movie about the Roman Empire.

She grimaced. 'No need to panic. It's not an emergency. I'm licensed.'

Barry proffered his most harmless smile. 'I wasn't even thinking of that.'

She didn't smile back. 'Then, what were you thinking?'

'I guess I was feeling sorry.'

To which her reaction was, alarmingly, to laugh.

Feeling betrayed and pissed-off, he grabbed the nearest can of vegetables (beets, he would later discover, and he hated beets) and handed it to Mr Morone with the can of Spam.

'That it?' Mr Morone asked.

'A six-pack of Schlitz,' he said, quite off the top of his head.

When he left the store with his dinner and the beer in a plastic bag, she was already outside waiting for him. 'I wasn't laughing at you, young man,' she told him, taking the same coolly aggrieved tone she'd taken towards the ice cream. 'I was laughing at myself. Obviously, I *was* asking for pity. So, if I should get some, I shouldn't be surprised, should I? My name's Madeline, but my friends call me Mad. You're supposed to laugh.'

'Mine's Barry,' he said. 'Do you drink beer?'

'Oh, I'm not drunk. I discovered long ago that one needn't actually drink in order to have the satisfaction of behaving outrageously.'

'I meant, would you like some now, with me? I've got a six-pack.'

'Certainly. Barry, you said? You're so *direct* it's almost devious. Let's go to my place. It's only a couple of blocks away. You see – I can be direct myself.'

Her place turned out to be four street-numbers away from his and nothing like what he'd been expecting, neither a demoralised wreck heaped with mouldering memorabilia nor yet the swank finicky *pied-à-terre* of some has-been somebody. It was a plain pleasant 1½-room apartment that anyone could have lived in and almost everyone did, with potted plants to emphasise the available sunlight and pictures representing various vanished luxuries on the wall, the common range of furniture from aspiring to makeshift, and enough ordinary debris to suggest a life being carried on, with normative difficulty, among these carefully cultivated neutralities.

Barry popped the tops off two beer-cans and Madeline swept an accumulation of books and papers off a tabletop and on to a many-cushioned bed. They sat down at the table.

'Do you know what it's called?' he asked. 'The disease you've got?'

'Sciatica. Which is more a disorder than a disease. Let's not talk about it, okay?'

'Okay, but *you'll* have to think of what we do talk about. I'm no good at coming up with topics for conversation.'

'Why is that?'

'No ideas. If other people have ideas I can bounce off them well enough, but all by itself my mind's a blank. I envy people like you who are able to start talking out of the blue.'

'Mm,' said Madeline, not unkindly. 'It's odd you should put it like that; it's almost a definition of what I do for a living.'

'Really, what's that?'

'I'm a poet.'

'No kidding. You can make a living by being a poet?'

'Enough to get by.'

Barry refused to believe her. Neither the woman nor her apartment corresponded with his preconceptions of poets and the necessarily indigent life they must lead. 'Have you ever published a book?' he asked craftily.

'Twenty-two. More than that, if you count limited editions and pamphlets and such.' She went over to the bed, rooted among the papers, and returned with a thin odd-sized paperback. 'This is the latest.' The front cover said in tasteful powder-blue letters on a ground of dusky cream: *MADELINE IS MAD AGAIN: New Poems by Madeline Swain.* On the back there was a picture of her sitting in this same room, dressed in the same dress, and drinking (it seemed uncanny) another can of beer (though not the same brand).

Barry turned the book over in his hands, examining the cover and the photo alternately, but would no more have thought of looking inside than of lifting Madeline's skirts to peek at her underclothes. 'What's it about?' he asked.

'Whatever I happened to be thinking at the moment I wrote each poem.'

That made sense but didn't answer his question. 'When do you write them?'

'Generally, whenever people ask me to.'

'Could you write a poem right now? About what you're thinking?'

'Sure, no trouble.' She went to the desk in the corner of the room and quickly wrote the following poem, which she handed to Barry to read:

A REFLECTION

Sometimes the repetition of what we have
just said will suggest a new meaning
or possibilities of meaning
we did not at first suppose to be there.
We think we have understood our words,
then learn that we have not,
since their essential meaning
only dawns on us the second time round.

'This is what you were thinking just now?' he asked sceptically.

'Are you disappointed?'

'I thought you'd write something about me.'

'Would you like me to do that?'

'It's too late now.'

'Not at all.'

She went to her desk and returned a moment later with a second poem:

AUBADE

I was sorry to hear
That you've got to be going.
But you're not?
Then I'm sorry to hear that.

'What does the title mean?' he asked, hoping it might modify the unfriendly message of the four short lines that followed.

'An aubade is a traditional verse-form that a lover addresses to his (or her) beloved at dawn, when one of them is leaving for work.'

He tried to think of a compliment that wouldn't be completely insincere. 'Heavy,' he allowed at last.

'Oh, I'm afraid it's not much good. I can usually do better. I guess I don't trust you enough. Though you're quite likeable – that's another matter.'

'Now I'm likeable! I thought' – he dangled the poem by one corner – 'you were just hinting that I should leave?'

'Nonsense. You haven't even finished your beer. You *mustn't* hold what I write against me. Poets can't be held responsible for what they say in their poems. We're all compulsive traitors, you know.'

Barry said nothing, but his expression must have conveyed his disapproval.

'Now, don't be like that. Treason is a necessary part of the job, the way that handling trash-cans is a part of being a garbage-man. Some poets go to a great deal of trouble to disguise their treacheries; my inclination is to be up front and betray everyone right from the start.'

'Do you have many friends?' he asked, needlingly.

'Virtually none. Do you think I'd go around talking to myself in grocery stores if I had friends?'

He shook his head, perplexed. 'I'll tell you, Madeline, it doesn't make sense to me. Surely, if you were nice to other poets, they'd be nice to you, on the basic principle of scratch-my-back.'

'Oh, of course. Minor poets do nothing else. They positively swarm. I'd rather be major and lonely, thank you very much.'

'Sounds arrogant to me.'

'It is. I am. C'est la vie.' She took a long throat-rippling sip of the Schlitz and set her can down on the table, empty. 'What I like about you, Barry, is that you manage to say what you think without seeming the least homicidal. Why?'

'Why do I say what I think? It's easiest.'

'No. Why are you so accommodating to me, when I'm being such a bitch? Are you looking for an endorsement?'

He blushed. 'Is it that obvious?'

'Well, as you don't appear to be either a mugger or a rapist, there had to be some reason you followed a dotty old woman home from her latest nervous breakdown. Let's make a deal, shall we?'

'What sort of deal?'

'You stay around and nudge some more poems out of me. I'm feeling the wind in my sails, but I need a muse. If you give me twenty good ideas for poems, I'll give you your endorsement.'

Barry shook his head. 'Twenty different ideas? Impossible.'

'Don't think of them as ideas, then. Think of them as questions.'

'Ten,' he insisted. 'Ten is a lot.'

'Fifteen,' she countered.

'All right, but including the two you've already written.'

'Done!'

'She sat down at her desk and waited for Barry to be inspired. 'Well?' she enquired, after long silence.

'I'm trying to think.'

He tried to think of what most poems were about. Love seemed the likeliest subject, but he couldn't imagine Madeline, at her age and with her temperament, being in love with anybody. Still, that was her problem. He didn't have to write the poem, only propose it.

'All right,' he said. 'Write a poem about how much you're in love with me.'

She looked miffed. 'Don't flatter yourself, young man. I may have inveigled you into my apartment, but I am *not* in love with you.'

'Pretend, then. And don't make it anything flip like that last one. Make it sad and delicate and use some rhymes.'

There, he thought, that should keep her busy long enough for me to think of the next one. He opened a second beer and took a meditative swallow. Did poets ever write poems about drinking beer? Or was that too general? Better to ask her to write about her favourite *brand* of beer, a kind of advertisement.

By the time she'd finished the sonnet about how much she loved him he had come up with all twelve other subjects.

1. A poem about her favourite beer, written as though it were an ad.

2. A poem in the form of a Christmas shopping list.

3. A poem embodying several important long-range economic forecasts.

4. A poem about a rabbit (there was a porcelain rabbit on one of the shelves) suitable to be sung to a baby.

5. A very short poem to be carved on the tombstone of her least-favourite president, living or dead.

6. A poem apologising to the last person she had been especially rude to.

7. A poem for a Get Well card to someone who has sciatica.

8. A poem analysing her feelings about beets.

9. A poem that skirts all around a secret she's never told anyone and then finally decides to keep the secret.

10. A poem giving an eyewitness account of something awful happening in Arizona, in February.

11. A poem justifying capital punishment in cases where one has been abandoned by one's lover. (This in its final expanded form was to become the longest poem in her next collection, 'The Ballad of Lucius McGonaghal Sloe', which begins

> I fell head over heels just four evenings ago
> With a girl that I'm sure you all know,
> But I couldn't hold her,
> And that's why I sold her,
> To Lucius McGonaghal Sloe.

and continues, in a similar vein, for another one hundred and thirty-six stanzas.)

12. A poem presenting an affirmative detailed description of her own face.

Prudently he didn't spring them on her all at once, but waited until she'd finished each one before telling her what the next had to be about. She didn't raise any further objections until he came to Number 8, whereupon she insisted she didn't have any feelings about beets whatsoever. He refused to believe her and to prove his point he cooked up a quick dinner on her hotplate of Spam and canned beets (it was rather late by then, and they were famished). Before she'd had three mouthfuls the poem started coming to her, and by the time she'd got it into final shape, five years later, it was far and away the best of the lot.

For the next many days Barry didn't speak to a soul.

He felt no need to communicate anything to anyone. He had his three endorsements – one from a poet who'd published twenty-two books – and he was confident he could have gone out and got three more a day if he'd needed to. He was off the hook.

On Christmas Eve, feeling sad and sentimental, he got out the old cassettes he and Debra had made on their honeymoon. He played them on the TV, one after the other, all through the night, waxing mellower and mellower and wishing she were here. Then, in February, when the world had once again refused to end, she did come home, and for several days it was just as good as anything on the cassettes. They even, for a wonder, talked to each other. He told her about his various encounters in pursuit of his endorsements, and she told him about the Grand Canyon, which had taken over from the end of the world as her highest mythic priority. She loved the Grand Canyon with a surpassing love and wanted Barry to leave his job and go with her to live right beside it. Impossible, he declared. He'd worked eight years at Citibank and accrued important benefits. He accused her of concealing something. Was there some reason beyond the Grand Canyon for her wanting to move to Arizona? She insisted it was strictly the Grand Canyon, that from the first moment she'd seen it she'd forgotten all about Armageddon, the Number of the Beast, and all the other accoutrements of the Apocalypse. She couldn't explain: he would have to see it himself. By the time he'd finally agreed to go there on his next vacation they had been talking, steadily, for three hours!

Meanwhile, Columbine Brown had been putting him off with a variety of excuses and dodges. The phone number she'd given him was her answering service, the address was an apartment building with guard-dogs in the lobby and a doorman who didn't talk, or listen. Barry was obliged to wait out on the sidewalk, which wasn't possible, owing to a cold wave that persisted through most of January. He left a message at the Apollo Theater, where the Pageant was held, giving three different times he would be waiting for her at Intensity Five. She never showed. By mid-February, he'd begun to be alarmed. Early one morning, defying the weather, he posted himself outside her building and waited (five miserable hours) till she appeared. She was profusely apologetic, explained that she *did* have his sticker, there was no problem, he shouldn't worry, but she had an appointment she had to get to – in fact, she was already late – and so if he'd come back tonight, or better yet (since she had to see somebody after the Pageant and didn't know when she'd be home) at this time tomorrow? Thoughtfully, she introduced him to the doorman so he wouldn't have to wait out in the cold.

At this time tomorrow Columbine made another non-appearance, and Barry began to suspect she was deliberately avoiding him. He decided to give her one last chance. He left a message with the doorman saying he would be by to collect his you-know-what at half-past twelve the next night. Alternately, she could leave it in an envelope with the doorman.

When he arrived the following evening, the doorman led him down the carpeted corridor, unlocked the elevator (the dogs growled portentously until the doorman said 'Aus!'), and told him to ring at door 8–C.

It was not Columbine who let him in, but her understudy, Lida Mullens. Lida informed Barry that Columbine had joined her husband in Wilmington, Delaware, and there was no knowing when, if ever, she might return to her post as Miss Georgia. She had not left the promised sticker, and Lida seriously doubted whether she had any left, having heard, through the grapevine, that she'd sold all three of them to an introduction service on the day they came in the mail.

With his last gasp of self-confidence Barry asked Lida Mullens whether *she* would consider giving him an endorsement. He promised to pay her back in kind the moment he was issued his own licence. Lida informed him airily that she didn't have a licence. Their entire conversation had been illegal.

The guilt that immediately marched into his mind and evicted every other feeling was something awful. He knew it was irrational, but he couldn't help it. The whole idea of having to have a licence to talk to someone was as ridiculous as having to have a licence to have sex with them. Right? Right! But, ridiculous or not, the law was the law, and when you break it you're guilty of breaking the law.

The nice thing about guilt is that it's so easy to repress. Within a day Barry had relegated all recollection of his criminal behaviour of the night before to the depths of his subconscious and was back at Intensity Five, waiting for whomever to strike up a conversation. The only person who so much as glanced his way, however, was Evelyn, the woman behind the refreshment-stand. He went to other speakeasies, but it was always the same story. People avoided him. Their eyes shied away. His vibrations became such an effective repellent that he had only to enter a room in order to empty it of half its custom. Or so it seemed. When one is experiencing failure, it is hard to resist the comfort of paranoia.

With only a week left till his temporary licence expired, Barry abandoned all hope and all shame and went back to Partyland with fifteen hundred dollars in cash, obtained from Beneficial Finance.

The MacKinnons were not on their blue settee, and neither Freddy the usher nor Madge of the green sofa could say what had become of them. He flopped into the empty settee with a sense of complete, abject surrender, but so eternally does hope spring that inside a quarter of an hour he had adjusted to the idea of never being licensed and was daydreaming instead of a life of majestic mysterious silence on the rim of the Grand Canyon. He rolled out the console and ordered a slice of pineapple pie and some uppers.

The waitress who brought his order was Cinderella Johnson. She was wearing levis and a tee-shirt with the word 'Princess' in big glitter-dust letters across her breasts. Her hat said, 'Let Tonight Be Your Enchanted Evening at Partyland!'

'Cinderella!' he exclaimed. 'Cinderella Johnson! Are you *working* here?'

She beamed. 'Isn't it wonderful? I started three days ago. It's like a dream come true.'

'Congratulations.'

'Thanks.' Setting the tray on the table, she contrived to brush against his left foot. 'I see you're wearing the same shoes.'

'Mm.'

'Is something the matter?' she asked, handing him the uppers with a glass of water. 'You look gloomy, if you'll forgive my saying so.'

'Sometimes it does you good to feel gloomy.' One of the pills insisted on getting stuck in his throat. Just like, he thought, a lie.

'Hey, do you mind if I sit down on your couch a minute? I am frazzled. It's a tremendous opportunity, working here, but it does take it out of you.'

'Great,' said Barry. 'Fine. Terrific. I could use some company.'

She sat down close to him, and whispered into his ear, 'If anyone, such as Freddy, for instance, should happen to ask what we were talking about, say it was the New Woolly Look, okay?'

'That's *Topic*'s feature story this week?'

She nodded. 'I guess you heard about the MacKinnons.'

'I asked, but I didn't get any answers.'

'They were arrested, for trafficking, right here on

this couch, while they were taking money from the agent that had set them up. There's no way they can wiggle out of it this time. People say how sorry they are and everything, but I don't know: they *were* criminals, after all. What they were doing only makes it harder for the rest of us to get our endorsements honestly.'

'I suppose you're right.'

'Of course I'm right.'

Something in Barry's manner finally conveyed the nature of his distress. The light dawned: 'You have *got* your licence, haven't you?' she asked.

Reluctantly at first, then with the glad uncloseted feeling of shaking himself loose all over a dance-floor, Barry told Cinderella of his ups and downs during the past six months.

'Oh, that is so terrible,' she commiserated at the end of his tale. 'That is so unfair.'

'What can you do?' he asked, figuratively.

Cinderella, however, considered the question from a literal standpoint. 'Well,' she said, 'we haven't ever really talked together, not seriously, but you certainly ought to have a licence.'

'It's good of you to say so,' said Barry morosely.

'So, if you'd like an endorsement from me ...?' She reached into her back pocket, took out her licence, and peeled off an endorsement sticker.

'Oh, no, really, Cinderella....'He took the precious sticker between thumb and forefinger. 'I don't deserve this. Why should you go out on a limb for someone you scarcely know?'

'That's okay,' she said. 'I'm sure you'd have done just the same for me.'

'If there is anything I can do in return ...?'

She frowned, shook her head vehemently, and then said, 'Well...maybe....'

'Name it.'

'Could I have one of your shoes?'

He laughed delightedly. 'Have both of them!'

'Thanks, but I wouldn't have room.'

He bent forward, undid the laces, pulled off his right shoe, and handed it to Cinderella.

'It's a beautiful shoe,' she said, holding it up to the light. 'Thank you *so* much.'

And that is the end of the story.

Noblesse Oblige

BRIAN GLANVILLE

'My gal Sal is the queen of all the acrobats,' declaimed John Bradford, gesturing with his left hand as he stirred hot cocoa with his right,

'Why, she's as clever as I don't know what.
She can shoot split peas out of her arsehole,
Do a double somersault, and catch them in her—

'No prizes offered! No prizes for guessing the last word!'

And he swung round to face the room, the cramped little kitchen, the mug of cocoa in his large right hand, his left hand stiffly and rhetorically extended, like a traffic policeman's, emerging from the grey braided sleeve of his dressing-gown. The other five men laughed with differing degrees of conviction. Peter Wallington, sitting in the middle of the kitchen on a hard-backed chair, looking at the floor, always withdrawn when he himself was not protagonist, merely grunted, his large, pale, doughy face distant and impassive. Plump Desmond Green, in spectacles, laughed loudly. George Aspall, also spectacled, gave no more than a token and unsmiling chuckle, his expression the habitual one of covert calculation. Pat Cullen laughed with boyish enjoyment, his teeth white and even as a movie star's. Loudest of all laughed Reg Cummings, his delighted cackle rising high above the rest. 'Knows a few, our John does!' he said, in his Bristol burr, bald and sly and cheerful. 'He's a boy, he is!'

The kitchen stood in a long brick bungalow, high on a hillside; the hillside and its pines were smothered and festooned with snow. The East Anglian night was very cold, but the kitchen was warm, even though an upper window, in conformity with sanatorium practice, was open. A tall grey paraffin-stove burned in a corner.

'Got any more, John?' Reg asked him, still laughing.

'No more frivolity,' said John, in his impeccably modulated voice, and sat down on a cane chair by the wall opposite the windows, facing Desmond, Reg and Pat. He was the largest man in the room, though Wallington was large, too: broad shoulders, broad back, with large firm features, a long, straight, narrow nose, a mouth wide but not full, a strong chin, a mitre of wiry fair hair. His eyes were large, too, and brown, steady and amused, like those of a quizzical dog. He tended to speak in asides, throwaways, crisply decisive but a little husky, given to succinct commentary, aphorism. It was easy to believe that, five years earlier, he had been a tank commander. It was equally easy to conceive of him as a fighter pilot, the captain of a torpedo-boat or, as Cullen had been, a paratrooper. There was an air about him at once patrician and vaguely archaic, like a monument in a fine state of repair, yet in danger of demolition. His ribaldry was as stylised as his courtesy, each kept perfectly in its own compartment.

'How many people *die* here in a year?' asked George Aspall in his thin plaintive voice.

There was an instant heavy silence till Reg Cummings asked, 'Why, aren't you feeling well, George? You look all right to me.'

'No,' said Aspall doggedly, 'what I mean is I think they'd hush it up. They wouldn't let you know. It don't *pay* them to let you know. It's bad for business.'

'Business?' said Wallington, raising his head to give him a saurian glance.

'A sanatorium's a business. A private sanatorium. It

stands to reason. If people didn't get TB they'd have to close down. People come here to be cured. If they die, it gets the place a bad name.'

'So you don't believe in anything as romantic as a sense of vocation?' asked John Bradford.

'What's that? The thing a nun has?'

'Broadly speaking, yes.'

'But a nun don't have to earn a living. A doctor has to make his living. Especially at a place like this.'

'*I* see,' said John, '*I* see. So the doctors might as well be selling soap.'

'They're selling health.'

'Very Shavian.'

'I might say that of Spence,' said Desmond. 'I'd never say it of Carlton Jones.' Spence, tall and temperamental, was the senior physician, Carlton Jones the amiable surgeon. 'Carlton Jones is a human being. He cares about you.'

'He's not a saint,' said Aspall. 'If you ask me, they enjoy it, surgeons.'

'I'll tell you who else enjoys it,' said Reg Cummings, 'that Annie. She's the one to put lead in your pencil.'

'She might put something else there, too,' said Aspall.

To this John Bradford did not react or respond; they might have been speaking in a foreign tongue. Annie was an Irish nurse, thin, dark and insinuating; her white cap, her all-white uniform lampooned virginity. The male nurses, too, wore white – white coats, as did the doctors. There was Nurse Ronnie Bowers, a local man, knowing and familiar, of whom John Bradford had said, 'With a bit more brain, that fellow would be a quarter-wit.' There was Nurse Arthur Field, who never smiled, and whose solemn brown eyes reflected a chronic bewilderment.

Big Staff Nurse Banks, a Yorkshirewoman whose calf-muscles stood out of her immense legs as she walked, like cannon-balls, wore a uniform of blue, adorned with many badges and ribbons. Blue, too, was the uniform of plump, sloppy, sentimental Nurse Davies, who was given to singing popular songs, and Flemish Nurse Devrindt, of legendary strength and efficiency with her kind, whiskery, leathery face. She worked in the Brick Block, where the thoracoplasty operations took place, where ribs were removed and patients did indeed sometimes die.

Nurse Brogan, who was Irish, too, and with her short red hair, her spectacles and her blotchy freckles looked like a truncated pantomime dame, wore pale green, with a white apron. When she gave injections into patients' rumps her hand shook like an inept darts-player's.

At the head of the hierarchy, the Matron of the sanatorium wore a long, dark-blue, pleated dress, tight in the waist, and a frilled white cap, a uniform indeed, uncompromisingly Victorian, Nightingalesque, imposing in its very obsolescence, the woman implacably subordinated to the role. It required conscious labour to separate the two, such was the aseptic briskness with which the Matron moved and behaved, comforted and rebuked, succoured and castigated, her formality of speech and smile and gesture. Only then could one see that she was a pretty and attractive woman, still below forty, for all the importance of her job. The success of her masquerade or of the uniform's disguise, might be gauged by the fact that no one seemed to know her name, her surname, let alone her Christian name. She was always 'Matron', the function smothering the individual, despite the delicate symmetry of her features, mouth and nose and chin, her high-boned, lightly freckled cheeks, the luminous humour of her grey eyes, the piquancy of her words and ways. Could there be a body there, beneath the blue dress, which rendered her as sexless as an angel, confining what must clearly be small breasts, constricting her throat with its high punitive collar? Was there some great petrifying grief in her past, a hero killed in the war? One would clearly never know. It *was* known that she had been an army nurse, had trained at one of the great London teaching hospitals, had been at the sanatorium for three years. Further than that, significantly, no one probed, nobody enquired, accepting her as somehow irreducible.

By the same token, she seemed invulnerable to the disease, the very idea of the disease, though it was an occupational hazard, striking down not only patients, but now a nurse, now a doctor.

Behind this barricade she appeared to exist with cool sufficiency, her private life unguessably private. The doctors treated her with punctilio; even Dr Spence would banter rather than bluster. The nursing staff deferred to her, the patients were unvaryingly respectful. They might joke with her, but the borderlines were drawn. She and John Bradford treated one another with a certain ritualised badinage.

'My dear Matron.'

'My dear Captain Bradford.'

They would meet once a week in the entrance hall of the main building at the weighing machine, a broad, old-fashioned wooden armchair whose weights the Matron would chink and clink – another ritual – displaying in the meantime sympathy, encouragement, a little humour, to the long line of those patients who came to be weighed, some patients dressed, some in their dressing-gowns, others in wheelchairs.

With John it was humour. 'There can never be too little of you, James,' he would announce to a younger patient who has lost a pound. Then, when it came to his own turn, he would sit down like a king, a hand on either arm of the chair. 'You may anoint me, Matron.'

'I shall *crown* you, Captain Bradford, if you aren't careful.'

At times, though very rarely, she would make her rounds of the hillside where the bungalow stood and the chalets with their white wooded walls, their two small identical sections, their glass doors, their iron bedsteads. John Bradford lived in a chalet on the highest level of the hill. He shared it with Desmond Green, who was a council clerk from Grimsby, worried endlessly about his future, treated John as an oracle and had been advised by Aspall to deal privately in contraceptives: 'As a matter of fact, Desmond I *do* know a good racket: French letters.'

'It's all right for you, John,' Desmond would say. 'You've got your Stock Exchange to go back to.'

'If I can,' said John. 'If they want me.'

He, like Desmond, had had a lung collapsed, an AP, necessitating periodic refills of air, through needles thrust between the ribs. 'I've no promise, you know. Nothing's been agreed. And, besides, you're on your feet an awful lot, out on that wretched floor. It may be a year, perhaps even two, before I'm fit again; if I'm ever fit again. Or ever willing.'

'Anything's better than sitting at a bloody desk, clerking for the rest of your life.'

'It's an imperfect world, my dear fellow.'

Each patient's day was scrupulously calibrated. There were, besides the bedridden, those who got up for lunch but not for dinner, those who got up for both, those all but refurbished few who were allowed up for breakfast. There were those who could walk down the straight white road from the sanatorium as far only as the first farm gate, three hundred yards away, those who could go as far as the golf-course, the railway-bridge, the village, and farther still over the flat green expanses of the countryside, through the plenitude of little villages with their neatly towered Tudor churches. There were those who languished in the Brick Block, awaiting or recovering from operations, their ribs torn out, their strength permanently diminished, those who hawked morosely into their sputum-mugs in the main building, those who lived rigorously on the hillside in huts with three sides, the fourth a mere tarpaulin.

John was well advanced towards release and recovery. He did not yet come down for breakfast but he was up for the rest of the day, walking as far as he wished in the afternoons, between the end of lunch and the communal tea, at which he would hand cups and plates about with punctilious diligence, dressed in his dark-blue brass-buttoned blazer, his cavalry-twill trousers, his Hawks Club tie. At other times he would wear jersey, thick, rough, woollen seaman's sweaters, with polo necks and discreet patterns, brown on white or grey.

Crossing the golf-course, John would invariably stop by the hedge which ran along the road, look with quick caution right and left, then, if there were no one in view, unbutton his trousers and urinate. 'If they see anything Nature didn't make, they can call a policeman.'

Then he would stride vigorously across the course, swinging a heavy wooden walking-stick, contemptuous of any golfers – 'The safest place is right in front of them' – sometimes, if he had company, bawling songs into the wind.

'The first lady forward, the second lady pass,
The third lady's finger up the fourth lady's arse.
The fifth lady *pas de deux*, the sixth lady, too.
The seventh lady's finger up the eighth lady's flue.'

Beside him there would sometimes walk Desmond Green, sometimes the Irishman Pat Cullen, sometimes James Branch, an eager pink-cheeked nineteen-year-old, puppyishly good-humoured, who asked endless questions about the war, cryptically answered. John talked little about it, even with Pat, who had been dropped at Arnhem and survived, while John's light armoured cavalry – 'mobile sardine-cans, my dear fellow' – had been advancing through Belgium.

Now and again, as they walked the roads, the fields, the golf-course or the sea-shore, one or the other would make some curt, almost reluctant, allusion – memory revived by the sight of barbed wire, a hunter with a gun, a clump of trees on a hill.

'Did you get drunk before you jumped?' John asked him once.

'Usually. Did they ever knock your tank out?' Cullen asked.

'Once south of Rome and once in Normandy.'

Then they would smile the wry ironic smiles of men who had escaped a violent death in war to be threatened by a squalid one in peace.

'I wish *I'd* been in the war,' sighed James, as they crunched across the stony beach, its pebbles shifting and slipping beneath their feet.

'You were well out of it, my dear boy, well out of it. An overrated pastime. One was either dead drunk or scared stiff.'

The sea was a bleak and sullen grey, James searched the beach for a flat stone, found one beside a pile of viscous brown seaweed, skimmed it across the water, and watched it bounce twice before it sank. 'Perhaps I wouldn't have got *this*,' he said.

'You might have got much worse. You'll recover. You've got time on your side.'

'So have you.'

'I'm nigh on thirty, my dear fellow.'

This he would say, quite frequently, with a curious kind of resignation, as though life, or at least youth, vanished at that age. Yet his bursts of cheerfulness continued. None, in what he called The Ablutions – the narrow wash-room in the bungalow, with its two yellow basins – was more buoyantly Rabelaisian.

'Take it in your hand, Mrs Murphy!' he would cry,

in a thick mock-Irish accent, his broad shoulders, his solid hairless chest bare, as he stood in his pyjama trousers, razor waving like a baton in his hand,

'Sure, 'tis the finest piece of mutton in the town!
It has hairs on its neck like a turkey,
And it spits if you rub it up and down!'

Whatever his detachment, communal living did not seem to oppress him. It was easy to divine in his past the earthy camaraderie of the school dormitory, the officers' mess.

'Damaged goods, Matron, damaged goods,' he said, with a slow shake of the head, when she visited him one day on her round, during the rest period preceding lunch. 'I'll never be A1 at Lloyd's again. My own fault. All that foolery in the war. Too much drink and not enough food.'

'What nonsense!' she laughed, perching lightly and gracefully on a chair opposite the end of his bed, her fingers linked together, pinkened by the cold. 'Stop feeling sorry for yourself!'

'I'm not sorry for myself, my dear Matron. I'm simply realistic.'

'You've learned the discipline. In a couple of years, you'll be able to forget about all this.'

'There's a great many things I'd like to forget.'

'Yes,' she said. 'We all would,' and continued to smile, looking at him a fraction longer than impersonality demanded, so that he, slightly startled, was the first to look away.

'You saw service, too,' he said.

'Oh yes. North Africa and Italy and France.' Her smile became anonymous again, a smile of stoicism and concealment.

'It must have been much harder,' he said. 'Putting people together. We were simply the idiots who got ourselves hit.'

'You'd be surprised how callous one can get.'

'Callous?' he said. 'Not you. I don't believe it.'

'Don't you know about us matrons?'

This time he did not look away from her smile.

'She likes you,' Desmond said to him.

'Me? Perfect rubbish.'

'Yes, she does. Why shouldn't she, anyway?'

When the two of them met again, it was on the golf-course. He was walking alone that afternoon, stick rhythmically swinging, turning off the road, through a gap in the hedge and up on to the golf-course, stopping to glance round, lean the stick against his side, unbutton his trousers, and proceed to urinate. At the suggestion of a sound behind him in the snow, he looked round sharply to his right, where there was another gap, saw no one there, whirled round again to his left, and there he saw the Matron, standing by the first gap, having clearly come in from the right and passed behind him, hands clasped inside her cloak, regarding him quite unembarrassed, smiling.

He was dumbfounded, quickly buttoning himself up again. 'My dear Matron!'

'My dear John!' she said, with great amusement.

'Completely unforgivable! I'd *ab*solutely—'

'No idea?'

'None whatsoever.'

'It might have been a perfect stranger.'

'I should have *preferred* it to be a prefect stranger.'

'I do see such things professionally, you know.'

'I know, I know, but.... Quite appalling. I can only apologise.'

'And I accept your apology,' she said; then, since she showed no signs of walking on, it was he who did so, saluting her with his stick, crying, 'Deplorable!' marching off at a frantic military pace, while she stood watching him and laughing.

Twice on the following day, when their paths crossed, he became formal and remote, twice she greeted him with cheerful cordiality, gaining a response of smothering propriety. '*Very* well, thank you, my dear Matron, exceedingly well.'

The following evening, she invited him to take sherry in her room. 'You're *sure*?' he asked, evidently startled.

'Quite sure.'

Her room, like herself, was at once austere and feminine, the severity of roll-top desk, high-backed varnished chair, shelves of nursing manuals, rows of files, charts and certificates, the general rigorous tidiness, relieved by small explosions of colour, pockets of fantasy: embroidered screens, a bright Victorian quilt on the bed, pampas grass in a deep jar, a row of small bright bottles on the dressing-table, a regiment of suits and dresses visible behind a blue velvet curtain hung on rings.

Photographs stood here and there; one of herself, much younger, in a sleeveless dress, smiling the same smile, arm in arm with a young man in the uniform of an army officer, his fair hair immaculately lotioned and combed. John registered this with a fractional lifting of the eyebrows. The portraits, in a twin leather frame, of a grey-haired man with cheeks like her own, a plumper middle-aged woman, were clearly her parents.

'My dear Matron ...,' John began.

'Stop calling me Matron,' she said, 'and if you dare apologise again I'll turn you out.'

'Well, then,' he said, and laughed. 'I *shan't* apologise, and I shall call you....'

'Diana.'

'Diana,' he said reflectively, suggesting that the task was difficult. 'Most classical, most appropriate.'

She took a bottle and two stemmed glasses from a gnarled wooden cupboard and poured out sherry.

'Very handsome of you, my dear ... Diana.'

'You've such marvellous manners,' she said,

laughing at him. 'I always imagine you in a powdered wig and knee-breeches.'

'I see!' he said. 'I'm an anachronism! Well, you may be right. I don't like now. I don't like this period. All grab and grasp. All rights and no duties. I see it here. I see it in this sanatorium.'

'We don't expect gratitude, least of all from TB cases.'

'I know what you mean. Things I did myself when I was bedridden. Things I said. One isn't fully in control.'

'Not even you?'

'Not even I.'

She smiled again, bent forward, and kissed him gently on the lips. 'Have you ever been married?' she asked.

'I?' he said, momentarily bemused. 'No, never married. Engaged once or twice. They changed their minds. Very wise of them. And you?'

She shook her head, suddenly withdrawn, which threw him, too, into a hiatus of silence. It was she who broke it. 'There are two of you, aren't there?' she said.

'Two?'

'You here, now; and you on the golf-course.'

'Dear, dear,' he said, with a burst of embarrassed laughter, 'that disgraceful episode.'

'So funny!' she said. 'I laugh every time I think of it,' and she did laugh, taking his hand, till he began to laugh as well, both of them laughing, looking at each other. Finally, he kissed her.

She liked him. The fact was quickly common property, whispered and savoured and anatomised in the Brick Block and the main block, in the corridor where patients waited anxious in their dressing-gowns for 'refills', in the dining-room with its manifold tables and its wizened head waiter, in the nurses' common room with its coal fire, its gas-rings and its mugs of tea and cocoa.

'You've made a hit with Matron, then!' cried Annie, the Irish nurse, as she made John's bed, looking up at him suggestively with her lewd dark eyes.

'I? You've been spending too much time in the cinema, Annie.'

'And where have *you* been spending time?'

The gossip flourished, feeding on itself, on the indolence of long frustrating days, on the Matron's own compact self-sufficiency.

They now met regularly. Each evening, after dinner, he would visit her for sherry. 'Is it wise?' he asked her. 'Is it fair?'

'Perfectly wise. Perfectly fair. It's such a damnable place for gossip.'

'Damn their gossip!'

This was the shape of it. She seemed far less concerned by any threat to her dignity than he; it was he who would break first from an embrace, he who would start back at any knock at the door, while she, reclining in her armchair, comfortable as a cat, would smile and call amiably, 'Come in!'

Alone with him, austerity melted into playfulness, the strait-laced uniform became a parody, a fancy dress. When she could, when it was her day off, she would put on other clothes: a pale-blue Angora jersey with a grey pleated skirt, a tailored suit in purple tweed. 'Very nice,' he would say, 'very nice, but I like you in uniform, too.'

'You like everything to be in uniform!'

It was she who suggested they should meet in Norwich. 'I've a weekend free. You've only a month left here. You could ask for leave to go to London.'

'And go to Norwich?'

'Yes.'

He was silent; then he said, 'Wouldn't it be foolhardy?'

'*Fool*hardy!' she echoed fiercely. 'It's *my* risk, *my* stupid reputation, *my* choice. Why must you always hide behind your blasted chivalry? Will you or will you *not* come to Norwich?'

'I shall come,' he said.

Asked for a weekend's leave, Dr Spence gave him a wolfish grin, said, 'Going to do something in the City?' and inscribed his temperature-chart for the three days 'On Parole.'

It was John who reached Norwich first, taking a taxi from the railway-station through streets whose snow was decomposing in the gutters into muddied slush, surprised, after the months of isolation, by the cars, the crowds, the myriad activity. At the Anglia Hotel, with its low ceilings, its chintz covers, its fussy cosiness, he took a double room in his own name and said he was expecting his wife.

It was mid-afternoon. The room was large and white-walled, a blue cloth counterpane over its marital bed, a wash-basin with brass taps in one corner, prints of old Norwich on the walls. He did not unpack his black leather grip but sat in an armchair reading *The Times*, restlessly turning the pages, until at last, on a single knock at the door, he leaped to his feet, strode across the room and let Diana in. Pink and smiling with delight, her face seemed transiently the face of the young girl in her photograph. She was wearing a grey, belted cloth overcoat, her ungloved hands were cold to his touch. When he kissed her she broke away, saying 'Now, now!' and flung the coat on to the floor.

She made love with an inventive passion, delighting in his body, in his potency, her own body small and firm and strong, her breasts tiny and conical with large resilient nipples. When she came, it was with an ecstatic spasm, her body arched with joy, 'Ah, ah, ah,' her eyes closed, her smile transported. Slowly the tautness went out of her body, her legs moved little by little down the bed, the smile became one of deep content, her eyes stayed shut. Propped on his hands, he hovered over her, looking at her with a grave solicitude.

She opened her eyes at last, running a finger lovingly down his cheek, his neck, his chest. 'I like you when you forget your ghastly good breeding!' she said.

By the time they dressed it had long been dark outside. 'Let's have dinner here!' she said. 'It's nice. They've a lovely panelled dining-room with doddery old waiters.'

'Do you think we should?'

'Oh, of *course* we should!' she said, shaking her hair out of her eyes, its darkness lightly touched with threads of grey. 'Can't you *ever* relax?'

He shrugged, inhaling deeply.

They went down to the restaurant, a long, low, twilit room, with a thick carpet, heavily draped windows, inglenooks, assiduous quiet waiters in tails. They ordered smoked salmon, then trout, followed by game-pie, and drank a bottle of Bordeaux. She chatted eagerly, often touched his hand, and they laughed continually.

They had just been given coffee in an array of jugs when Reg Cummings walked into the dining-room with Annie. There was a moment's mutual petrifaction, then Annie, with a high half-smothered giggle, nudged Reg, who grinned in turn, took her by the arm and led her out again, he in loud baggy checks, she in a short and sleeveless crimson dress, from which her wiry, brown, bare arms extended like tendrils.

Diana and John sat in silence, Diana now pale as paper, John with a sombre stoicism. 'If it hadn't been *that* little whore,' she said at last.

'It's my fault,' he said, 'it's entirely my responsibility. Quite unforgivable.'

'Shut up!' she said, and he looked at her astonished. 'There's no responsibility to take, and if there were it would be mine as much as yours. More than yours. *I'm* in the responsible position.'

He dropped his gaze. 'As you wish,' he said.

She grasped him fiercely by the wrist. 'Come upstairs!' she said. 'I want to go upstairs!'

In the bedroom she made love with almost violent abandon, stroking and sucking him into life after each orgasm, as though the night was sure to be her last.

'You can't go back,' he said next morning.

'Why not? Why can't I go back? How dare they judge me! *You* needn't go back, if you feel you can't face it.'

'Of course I shall go.'

'Of course, of course, of course!' she mocked him. 'It's your duty, isn't it? Protecting my good name! Go if you want to. Don't if you don't!'

He gave what was almost a sigh and said, 'I want to.'

They travelled together, side by side in the narrow third-class compartment with its fly-blown dingy cushions, speaking very little, her hand resting in his. Seen through the window, the disappearing fields were brilliant with sun and snow, the sky a vivid icy blue, the hedgerows rimed, as spiky as wire, the flat country stretching out of sight like a white desert. She seemed much happier than he, looking at him now and then with a devoted smile, to which he would respond very slowly, as though fighting through clouds of despair.

At the little local station he kissed her, put her into the solitary taxi and said it would be better if he walked. She drove off cheerfully, turned to wave to him through the rear window, till she was out of sight around a curve.

He walked slowly, carrying his black leather bag, the snow crisp and friable beneath his feet, the air very sharp, no one to be seen in the surrounding fields or on the golf-course when he cut across it, the deeper snow now sliding damply into his shoes. The sanatorium and its buildings, too, were silent, as if deserted or enchanted, in the rest hour before lunch. He climbed the high steep hill to his chalet.

Desmond Green was lying on his bed, earphones on

his head, listening to the radio. Seeing John he looked surprised, his face mimed a question, but John merely lifted a hand and went into his own room. He threw the case into a corner and sat down on the bed, head resting in his hands. He had not moved when, half an hour later, there were brusque footsteps in the snow, the door burst open, and Dr Spence stood above him in his white linen coat, stethoscope around his neck like a talisman, his long brown face transfigured by rage.

'Get out!' he said. 'Leave at once! You've betrayed my trust! You've broken your word to me! You've compromised this sanatorium!'

John heavily raised his head and regarded him. 'You're quite right, Doctor,' he said. 'I'm afraid you're perfectly justified. I'd like to apologise, and I accept complete responsibility.'

'Damn your apologies! Just get your things together and go!'

He turned on his heel, grasped the handle of the glass-panelled door as if to slam it, then on an afterthought released it, leaving the door open to the cold. When his quick heavy footsteps could no longer be heard Desmond Green appeared, his moon face melancholy. 'I'm sorry, John,' he said.

'Ha! You've already heard, have you? The bush telegraph is working as well as ever.'

'I'm afraid so.'

'And with something to work on at last! No need to invent! No need to concoct! Caught *in flagrante delicto*! What a banquet!'

He took down from the top of the plain brown wooden wardrobe a pale-blue leather suitcase, much scratched and battered, and began to pack.

'Can I help you?' Desmond asked.

'No. No, thank you, my dear fellow. I'd rather be on my own, if you don't mind. Entirely my own fault. Entirely my own doing. Quite inexcusable.'

He had just closed the case when there were further

footsteps in the snow, lighter this time. At the sound of them he turned quickly, almost eagerly, to see that it was Diana. She was wearing her uniform again. Her face was taut and very pale. 'How dare he throw you out like this!' she said.

'I'm afraid he has every right to.'

'Right! He has *no* right! I've told him so. He has responsibilities to you as a patient. He's a pompous, pretentious, conceited fool. I've told him that, too. And I've resigned!'

'I see,' he said, in a very low voice, looking down at the case, and she took his arm.

'For Heaven's sake!' she said. 'There are other places, other countries, other jobs. You don't think I meant to stay here the rest of my life, do you?'

At this he turned to her and said, 'I should like to marry you, Diana.'

She looked up at him in silence, bemused at first, incredulous, then suddenly began to laugh, louder and louder. 'I could slap you!' she cried. 'I could shake you! You idiot! How dare you try to make an honest woman of me?'

'Leaving you like this,' he said. 'The filth, the gossip – it's unbearable.'

'For you or for me? *I* can bear it! A lot of chattering patients! A few venomous little nurses! A conceited doctor! I'll stay a month and then I'll come to London. We can be together.'

'And you'll marry me?'

'*No!*' she cried. 'I'll never marry you!'

She rose on tiptoe, kissed him on the mouth, then hurried out of the chalet, along the snowy path with her quick, short, functional strides, down the steep descent among the pines.

He walked out after her to follow her progress down the hill, her compact figure, in its white cap and blue cloak, appearing and disappearing through the trees. It was the first time he had ever heard her singing.

The Hat on the Letter 'O'

NICHOLAS HASLUCK

THE POSTCARD? What's it doing up there? You want to know? Listen. Do me one favour. Don't get me started on the postcard. Not at this hour of night. Not unless you can stay for another drink. The postcard! What a question. What an absolutely hysterical question. See that? Exactly. The crystalline tear and the weary smile. A postcard-from-abroad type smile.

But, since we're on the subject, tell me one thing. Have you ever heard of a man fastening a seat-belt on a woman without touching her once? You know – leans across, finds the clip deep down beside the seat on the far side, then the buckle part, and snaps them together, and tightens up until you can hardly breathe. And all the time never touches you once. Not even with a fraction of a finger-tip. I mean, how depressing can it get? I use toothpaste and talc and everything. And here's this *male* crawling all over the place on tippy-toe fingers. And I'm sitting there like the plague.

But it's obvious why. Let's face it. The whole thing was a fiasco from the start. An absolute fiasco. You don't have to be sober to see that. It sticks out ten miles. The big relationship. Honestly, it was doomed from the word go.

'You must get out more, darling,' Mother says. 'You've got to start afresh.' Can't you just hear her saying it? In that teeny-weeny 'it's-none-of-my-business-but-be-*reasonable*' voice? Of course you can. She's predictable. Absolutely predictable.

What chance did I have? Next thing, I'm togged up

in whites and handing out pikelets at the tennis club. You know what Mother's like. The whole thing was hysterical. Well, for God's sake, I don't have to tell *you*. You know what she's like from way back.

I can just see her. Down there with that secretary man. Laying it on with a front-end loader. 'You see, I have this daughter. And her husband died tragically. And she's been looking a little peaky. And we've all been telling her she must get out in the sunshine – now that her husband is tragically dead.' Then, next thing, the tennis togs and the pikelets.

And the washing-up. Let's not forget the washing-up entirely. Let's not forget that. The tea they used to drink down there. Mopped it up by the bucketful. But that reminds me. What do people usually say when someone comes to their house? 'Would you like to have a wash?' Or do they say, 'Would you like to wash up?'

Do you know what happened the first time I went over to his flat? The night of the seat-belt? Lucky I can talk to you freely. Do you know what happened?

We get to his place. OK? He helps me unbuckle. Still the plague. Then he fumbles round with the keys and everything and we get inside. On with the lights. Every light in the place. And do you know what he says? Absolutely the first thing he says? 'Would you like to wash up?' No kidding. That's the first thing he says.

So I'm standing there. Under the arc-lights. And he's helping himself off with his coat and so on. Well, I know I'm meant to be dumb. But what would you think? The place looks like a pig-sty and he's asking me to wash up. Ash-trays everywhere. Sink chock-a-block with plates. Well, it wasn't that bad, actually. But it wasn't good. Not when you're standing there in your first new dress in fifty years. And after the seat-belt and everything.

What sort of a nerve has he got? That's what I kept saying. Not out loud, of course. But that's what I was thinking. Who is this man? Paul Newman? The first time out with him on a Saturday night and you're over at his place to do the washing-up. And he's pottering about in the doorway looking polite and everything. As though he's done you a big favour.

Of course, it was all a mistake. He's a Canadian. That's what they say over there. 'Would you like to wash up?' Meaning: Would you like to slip into the loo before we have a drink? We sorted it all out after a couple of minutes. A couple of long hard minutes. Apparently, that's what they're used to saying, the Yanks. Or the Canadians, I should say. Well, in fact, the French Canadians. That's where he turned out to be from. From Quebec.

See how he's spelt his name on the postcard? We all called him John. But in fact you don't say it that way. You say 'Jean'. Just like that. 'Jean.' And see that. I'll tell you a funny thing about that. Believe me, I shudder when I think back on it. What a night. What an absolutely hysterical night. Tottering from one fiasco to another. First the seat-belt. Then the propositioning on the washing-up. Honestly, I couldn't take a point. The number of incredible things you're supposed to know about a Canadian. Or a Quebecian – or whatever you call them.

You see, after the washing-up thing we had a drink. And got talking. OK? And you know how it is when something silly happens? It made it all that much easier. Kind of relaxed things. So we were just sitting there nattering about this and that. Nothing important really. He had a look at my new outfit and said it was great. And I told him he had a nice place except that it looked like a pig-sty. Well, what was I meant to say? It didn't look like anything else. And he didn't mind anyhow. Just laughed. And looked a bit sheepish.

In fact, it was obvious he wasn't the kind of person to be bothered by what people said about his place. You know, he was always one of those shambling-around kind of men. I mean, he didn't smoke a pipe or anything but he had that kind of look. Sort of 'wise' but sort of dumb all at once. You know what I mean? Not quite there. Thinking about something else half the time. You could tell he didn't mind what he did with himself.

Now, where was I? That's right: the pig-sty. So after that it was more or less agreed that he'd go down and get some hamburgers while I did the washing-up. Which I did. And you should have *seen* the gangrene floating round inside his tea-pot. Or is it penicillin? You know, a great scum of it. Floating round like a giant lily. All green and furry. Ugh. I practically choked. But I didn't tell him that. Didn't have the heart to. Not when he came back with his hamburgers. Laying them out on plates as if they were home-made meringues or something.

Anyhow, to cut a long story short, we polished off the hamburgers. And somehow the conversation came back to this thing about languages and different customs between countries and so on. And, honestly, I'm not sure how we got talking how we did. I was just drowsing away there and nodding and everything. Like you do when a chap gets started on something. Cricket or skin-diving or whatever it is. Just sort of dreaming away. Getting a bit bored actually. When all of a sudden – and I can remember it as clearly as yesterday – with a really mournful voice he says, 'All my life I've been bearing the burden of a circumflex.'

Wow, I thought to myself. This is it. Things are starting to move. We're getting down to bed-rock. This could be something. I mean, let's face it, I still had the seat-belt hanging over me. But this mournful voice. Things were beginning to perk up. The confession, the sympathy and then – well, anything.

So I thought: OK. Let's see where it leads. Let the thing unfold. He's been circumflexed. He's been bearing the burden all his life. And he's telling it to *me*. I mean, I know I'm meant to be dumb. But, frankly, it sounded like a terribly personal statement. After all, I'm the mother of children. I know what they do to boys out here.

So I said (you know, nice and relaxed), 'Oh, yes.' Just like that. Nothing more. No panic or anything. Just 'Oh, yes.' Absolutely casual. Took a sip of my drink. Lit a cigarette. Something like that.

Then it all started to go off the rails. He comes back and says something like 'At school I used to have this teacher who called it "putting a Chinese hat on the letter 'o'".'

I nearly wet myself. I mean, these days everyone's on the pill and so on. But how would you know what they're doing in *Canada*?

'Oh, yes,' I said, again. 'Oh, yes.' Nearly choking. Who is this man? I kept thinking. This Quebecian. First the seat-belt. And now his teacher's putting a Chinese hat on the letter 'o'. His teacher! What's he got to do with it? What sort of a school was that, anyhow? Jesus. Let's get out of here, I thought. The man's a fruit. Why does it always happen to me?

Which reminds me – did I tell you about the guy with the gammy leg? The one Mrs Parsons rang up about? Just after the tennis club had flopped. You know, rang up that time and said her cousin was down from the bush. Lovely bloke and everything. Just my type. Then one minute later she's on my porch with this sandy-haired little fellow who opens the screen door and walks in – step-donk, step-donk, step-donk. Like that. And sits down with his leg out in front of him. Actually, he was a bit slow up top, too. Didn't I tell you about him?

That's the trouble. You just don't *know* what's been going on. Let's face it. I could write a book. An absolutely hysterical work of art. The problems. The pressure from all sides. That's how it got started with

John. The 'relationship', I mean – if you can call it that.

You see, about the time of the tennis club thing, my brother-in-law was working out at Harper's in marketing. And he and my sister kept telling me about this Yank. And then my mother came in and said I should meet him. Like I said, teeny-weeny voice: 'You can't just sit around at home, darling. You've got to start afresh.' Well, you know what she's like from way back.

Anyhow, by the time she came into the picture, I practically hated this man. This *American.* Everybody talking about him. Sweet man. Very 'natural'. Goes to the hockey on Saturdays. I mean, for heaven's sake. I could see from the way they were pushing him that he must be either a step-donk man or a complete nobody. I mean, if he was any good, he wouldn't be available, would he?

Do you know what happened? This sounds crazy, I know. When my brother-in-law brought him round – you know, more or less pushed him through the door – I was sitting there ready to hate him. Had it all bottled up inside. The sarcasm and everything. 'I once saw a film about Alcatraz,' I was going to say. 'Have you watched any hockey in Alcatraz?'

But it turned out he wasn't the sort you could say that to. Not really. With his hair all plastered down and shaking hands and being polite and everything. Anyway, he wasn't an American. He was a French Canadian. Besides, I quite liked the look of him. For once in my life, I kept my mouth shut for five minutes. Sat there like a sea-anemone. Peeping out of my shell. Do sea-anemones have shells? Well, whatever it is with a shell, I was inside it peeping out. Looking him over. Not that he would ever stand out in a crowd or anything. But he just seemed to have these friendly eyes. And quite sexy, too, in a quiet sort of a way. All right, so I've got a mind like a drain. I know it. But what are you meant to do? Sit there and say, 'Have you watched any hockey in Alcatraz lately?' I have instincts, too, don't I?

Anyhow, to cut a long story short, he started coming round on weekends. Played with the kids out in the garden. Took them swimming and off to the movies. To tell the truth, I don't know that I went for *that* in a big way. It kept me awake some nights. He was spending so much time with the girls, I couldn't help wondering what he was up to. Who was he after? Them or me?

All right. I've got a mind like a drain. I know it. I've already admitted it. I have a *vile* mind. OK? But you read about cases like that all the time. What about that girl up at Wangara? How do you think her parents must have felt? Inviting him in and everything. I mean, what are you meant to do without a husband? Sit back and watch your daughter get raped?

It was wild imagination, I admit it. Absolutely no cause for suspicion. None whatsoever. But, let's face it, I was going through a difficult stage. But I can tell you – for a time there, I was watching him like a hawk.

But nothing happened. And that was a problem, too. I mean, honestly. What was he coming round for? Good manners are terrific. I've got nothing against good manners. I'm all for them. If there's one thing I hate it's waiters cleaning their nails with a fork. But what, in fact, was he coming round here for all the time? What was he after? Never made a pass at me. Never tried anything. Never asked me out. No signs of jealousy. Well, to be fair, the only other fellow hanging round at the time was the step-donk man, and you wouldn't worry much about him.

So there it was. Nothing. The step-donk man and John. Or 'Jean' as you're meant to say it.

And then the seat-belt and the circumflex. Do you know what a circumflex turned out to be? You want to find out? See that. See that little angle above his surname? That little hat on the letter 'o'? That's a circumflex. Honestly. *That* is a circumflex. I could have wept. He sat there spelling out his name in capital letters and showing me all those other things – ay-graves and accents. They could have been specks of smallpox for all I cared. *And* I did a second lot of washing-up – with never a finger laid upon me. And that's including fastening the seat-belt on the way home.

'Jean' as you're meant to say it. The big relationship. And he only ever kissed me once. That's all. Just once. Not long before he left. And, if you want the truth, it was more me kissing him than him kissing me. Just to show him that it could be done. And now – the postcard.

Do you want to know something? And this sounds crazy, I know. But let's face it. I've missed him. Truly missed him. Shambling about in the garden and off to his hockey and all. Do you think that's possible? Knowing me?

I don't know what to think. I never found out whether he liked me. I think he did. I hope he did. He must have to some extent. He kept coming round. Perhaps I scared him off. Perhaps I was looking peaky. I know I talk too much. But how can you stop being what you are? He was such a gentle man, really. With his friendly eyes and handshaking and everything. A shy man, I suppose. Perhaps we never got to know each other properly.

But look at that little sketch he's done. Since that night at his flat, it's always been a joke between us. Any time he left a note for me he did one of those. Like a signature. A little round man with a Chinese hat on. Chopping some wood or going off with the kids. It's a bit smudged, but you can see that the little man's meant to be climbing on board a boat. And underneath he's written, 'Au revoir.' Meaning 'Until we meet again.'

But *you* know what that means in English from way back. Remember how they always closed off that programme on Tuesdays? The one we followed for a while? But I'm not starting that. Not at this hour. No, I'm keeping right away from that. I know what Mother would say. But how can you help it? How can you keep away from it? How can you stop thinking about someone out there in the darkness? And things happening to them you don't even know about. And changing them. And bringing them down. And time going by.... That's the thing that scares me. That one night you'll come back. But when I open the door it won't be you. It won't be a young man there. It'll be someone grey and beaten down coming in with an awkward smile. And walking to me – step-donk, step-donk, step-donk. And there'll be no starting afresh.

A Crush on Doctor Dance

SHIRLEY HAZZARD

WHEN Rupert Thrale was thirteen and had trouble with his back, his mother took him to a new hospital across the river. After the X-rays had been studied, it was again Grace Thrale who sat beside him in a waiting-room while he turned pages of a book on marsupials and tested a loose green rubber tile with the toe of his school boot. When, at the name of Thrale, they got up together to be shown to a doctor's empty office, they walked with arms touching. And, as they sat alone beside a desk, Mrs Thrale leaned forward out of her anxiety and kissed the boy; and the door opened.

The man who came in saw the mother bending forward, her arm extended on a chair-back, her throat curved in helpless solicitude, her lips to her son's hair which palely mingled with her own. In the next instant she turned and looked; and Rupert, getting to his feet, disowned her caress.

What Grace Thrale saw was a solid man of about thirty in Nordic colours – high-complexioned, blue-eyed, bright-haired, and dressed in white – standing at an open door.

The tableau was brief; but even the boy remembered it.

The three of them sat at the desk, and the young doctor said, 'Don't worry.' He put a row of photographs up on a metal rack and lit them: the notched segments, the costal arcs, the grey knuckled frame of a bare existence with its deathly omen. 'These are what we call the dorsal vertebrae.' He pointed with a pencil; and Grace Thrale looked at her son's mortality – all the respiring tissue blazed away, all that was mobile or slept, could resent or relish. It was as if she stared at an ossified remnant in a child's grave.

There was to be a corrective operation – which was delicate, infrequently performed, and involved a rod of stainless steel. It did not affect growth. 'You'll be better than new, I promise.' The doctor addressed himself in this way to the boy, without heartiness, in a low clear voice and slight Scots accent, including the mother by a filament of experience which was almost tender. His face, in its revealing colour and kindness, might in another era have been beautiful. His hair glowed, gold enough to be red.

When they were leaving, he told Grace she should make an appointment to come with her husband. 'We should talk it over with the surgeon.'

The boy's father, Christian Thrale, was about his country's business, conferring at Dar es Salaam. Grace would come alone on Thursday.

At the door there was a projecting sign: *Angus Dance, MD*.

On Thursday he lit the photographs and showed with the pencil. He said it was tricky but would be all right. They had the best man in London to do the job. Grace Thrale sat side by side with Angus Dance to look at the plates, and, handling one of them, left a tremulous print of humid fingers. When the surgeon arrived, Dance got up and stood in the sun by the window, where he was white and gold, a seraph, a streak of flame.

Grace told him that her husband was coming home, to be present for the operation.

'You'll be seeing my colleague. I'll be on leave that week.' He saw she was disturbed. 'Just for a few days.' When the surgeon left them, Dance sat to fill out his portion of a form. He told her he was going to his parents' house, near Inverness.

'What's Inverness like these days?'

'Oh – like everywhere – full of Japanese.' Reading over the form, he said, 'We're neighbours. I see you're in the Crescent. I live around the corner, in the place that's painted blue.'

They agreed they did not like the shade. Grace said she often walked past the building, taking the short cut through the brick passage – which, originally reserved for pedestrians, was now abused. She knew he said conventional things to calm her; and was calmed by his humane intention.

The Doctor said, 'Rupert will run me down there one day on his bike and I'll be a cot case.' He gave her back the form and touched her sleeve. 'You'll be anxious. But there is no need.'

The operation went so well that Christian Thrale was back at Dar es Salaam in a matter of days. The boy would be in hospital a month or so. Grace came every morning and afternoon, bringing comic books, a jigsaw, clean pyjamas. There was a cafeteria where she had lunch.

'How was Inverness?'

Doctor Dance was carrying a tray. 'The gateway to the Orient. I'm glad Rupert's doing so well.' His upright body gave a broad impression, both forcible and grave. He had short muscular arms, on which the hair would be red.

They sat down together and Grace conveyed Christian's gratitude all the way from Tanzania, even bringing out a letter. Relief gushed from her in forms of praise: the nurses were so kind, the surgeon, the therapist from Karachi. Sister Hubbard was a saint, and Rupert would be spoiled beyond repair. She then said, 'Well – why should you hear this in your time off?'

Her light hair was sculpted down from a central parting and fell in wings over her ears. Once in a while she would touch it, a ring glinting on her raised hand. Her nails were of a housewifely length, unvarnished. 'What about your journey?'

He said he always took the train. His parents lived an isolated life, but now had the telly. The house, which was in the Black Isle, was always cold, not only from heatlessness but from austerity. 'They like it bare. Predictably enough, my sister and I tend to clutter.' There was only one picture in the house: 'A framed photograph of the *Tirpitz*, which was sunk the day I was born. Or at least the news came that forenoon that they had sunk it.' His sister was also a doctor, and lived in Edinburgh.

Grace pictured the old crofters in the stark house uttering monosyllables like 'aye' and 'wee' and 'yon'; the maiden sister, a ruddy, tweedy pediatrician called, in all likelihood, Jean. 'They must miss the two of you.'

'My father still does consultant work He's an engineer. Then, I run up fairly regularly. And Colette is going to them for Easter. It's really harder for her, since she's married, with a family.'

That evening Grace asked at a dinner-party, 'Does anyone remember what year we sank the *Tirpitz*?'

It happened that Grace Thrale and Doctor Dance spoke every day. There were the X-rays to light up and look at – each of these tinged with the bloom of deliverance; there was Rupert's bedside, there were the corridors and the cafeteria. Once they stayed ten minutes talking on a stair. They soon dispatched the neighbourhood topics – the abused brick passage, the hideous new hotel nearby that took groups – and Grace found out that Angus Dance was divorced from a student marriage, voted Liberal, had spent a year in Colombia on an exchange programme, and kept a small sailing boat at Burnham-on-Crouch. He had done prison visiting at Wormwood Scrubs, but now lacked the time. One day he had a book on his desk, about the Brontës.

Mentioning his marriage, he said, 'Young people aren't doing that so much now.' Younger than she, he already considered himself an elder.

Grace told him how her parents had died in the wreck of a ferry when she was four. Next – so it seemed, as she came to relate it – there had been Christian. Recounting these things, she felt her story was undeveloped, without event; years were missing, as from amnesia, and the only influential action of her life had been the common one of giving birth. The accidental foundering of her parents had remained larger than any conscious exploit of her own, and was still her only way to cause a stir.

This vacancy might have affected growth. Compared with his variousness, she was fixed, terrestrial; landlocked, in contrast to his open sea.

These exchanges with Doctor Dance were Mrs Thrale's first conversations. With Christian there was the office, there were the three children, there the patterns and crises of domestic days. She had not often said, 'I believe', 'I feel'; nor had felt the lack. Now beliefs and feelings grew delightful to her, and multiplied. Between visits to the hospital, she rehearsed them: she held imaginary discourse with Angus Dance, phantasmal exchanges in which Grace was not ashamed to shine. There was a compulsion to divulge, to explain herself, to tell the simple truth. The times when she actually sat by him and looked at X-ray plates generated a mutual kindliness that was the very proof of human perfectibility. After these occasions there was consciousness of exertion – a good strain such as the body might feel from healthful unaccustomed action.

One day, passing a paper from hand to hand, their fingers touched; and that was all.

'I suppose', said Grace Thrale, 'that Angus was always a Scots name.'

'It's a version of Aeneas.'

She could not recall what Aeneas had done, and thought it better not to ask.

He was changing her. She wished more than anything to match his different level of goodness – his sensibility that was precise as an instrument, yet with a natural accuracy; his good humour that was a form of generosity; his slight and proper melancholy. It was virtue she most desired from him, as if it were an honour he could confer. He could make an honest woman of her.

The bare facts of Mrs Thrale's love, if enumerated, would have appeared familiar, pitiful and – to some – even comical. Of this, she herself was conscious. It was the sweetness that was unaccountable.

Because the condition struck her as inborn, she raked her experience for precedent. She dwelt on a man she had known long ago, before her marriage – a moody schoolteacher who often broke appointments or came late, and over whom she had suffered throughout a cold summer. Only the year before, she had heard he was now farming in Dorset, and had looked up his name in the telephone directory. He provided no prologue to Angus Dance. In contrast to the schoolteacher, on the other hand, Christian had appeared a model of consideration, a responsible lover whose punctuality had from the start prefigured matrimony. Angus Dance had no precursor.

Grace put the end of a pen between her lips. Hugh, her middle son, said, 'Why do you look that way?'

'I'm thinking what to tell Daddy.'

At night she was alone with Angus Dance when she lay down solitary in the dark with her arm half-clasped about her body. She thought that Christian would soon return from Dar es Salaam. The knowledge that he would at once make love to her brought mere acceptance.

The week after Rupert came home from hospital, Mrs Thrale ran into Doctor Dance in the street. They met at a site of road repairs, and could hardly hear each other for the pneumatic drill. Grace stared at his clear, hectic skin and tawny head, his noonday colours, while concrete particles exploded and the pavement thrilled. Consciousness shivered also, on some inward Richter scale.

'Let's get out of this.' Dance went through a motion of taking her elbow but did not in fact do so. They were both going to the cake-shop, and agreed that the woman there was grumpy but the *croissants* good. When they crossed at the corner Grace said, 'We all miss you.' She heard this speech turn coy with trepidation, and a little tic started up in her cheek. He smiled: 'Now, that's going too far.' But added, 'I miss you all, too.' Saying 'all' both made it possible and detracted: a pact, scrupulously observed.

In the shop Grace had to wait for the seedcake. Angus Dance shook hands. 'Doctors are always overdue somewhere. I hope we meet again.'

When he had gone out, the grim woman behind the counter said, 'So he's a doctor, is he? He has a lovely face.'

When Christian praised the seedcake, Grace said, 'I got it from that nice woman at the corner.'

Every spring the Thrales gave a party – drinks and little things to eat. They called this decorous event 'our smash'. Grace went over her question in silence: I would like to invite that young doctor. We might ask Rupert's doctor, who lives practically next door. What about asking that Doctor Dance, who was super with Rupert?

To the question as ultimately phrased, Christian responded, 'Good idea.' He had it in mind to ask someone very senior from his department, and supposed a doctor would mix.

Grace telephoned the hospital. Dance knew her voice: 'Hello.' He did not say 'Mrs Thrale', and had never done so. He wrote the date of the party, and six to eight. 'Is it a special occasion?'

'It's my birthday. Not that we tell people.'

She had a new dress that displayed her breasts. Christian said, 'Isn't it a bit bare?' He traced the outline of black silk with his finger on her flesh. 'Happy birthday, Grace darling.'

Although they had a couple from Jamaica to do the drinks, it was Grace who opened the door to Angus Dance. Before entering, he bent and kissed her cheek, murmuring 'Birthday.' He gave her a little packet, which was later found to contain lavender water. Grace trembled under the astonishing kiss, from which she turned away with the male impress of jacket indelible on her silk and female arms. When Christian came over from the foot of the stairs, discarding his party face for the serious theme of Rupert, she moved back into the curve of the piano, where Dance soon joined her.

'Who plays?'

'I do.' For once she did not add, 'My sole accomplishment.' He leaned to look at stacked music. She had put the Chopin on top to impress. She saw him turn the sheets with deliberate large hands; she watched his almost spiritual face. Authority had passed from him in this amateur setting, and his youth was a blow, a disappointment. Authority had in fact passed to her. She presided, a matron, over her household, her associates, her charming children: mistress of the situation.

She did not know how to address him now that he was disestablished. At the hospital the nurses had called him 'Doctor', as women with a family will call their own husbands 'Father' or 'Daddy'.

They spoke about the community centre, and Grace told him the art show would open on Sunday. Dance said, 'I might look in.'

Rupert appeared with Dance's whisky, and other

guests were introduced. In an oval mirror they had bought in Bath she saw the room, tame with floral charm and carpeted, like England, wall to wall in green. And herself, in this field of flowers – practically indistinguishable from cushions and curtains, and from ornaments that, lacking temperament, caused no unrest. In the mirror she could see, rather than hear, her husband saying 'Let's face it', and watch her eldest son, Jeremy, blond and beloved, behaving beautifully. She saw the rings on her fingers, and a bracelet that was insured. Look as she might, she could not see Angus Dance in that mirror (he had been taken to the dining-room for a slice of the ham), and knew she never would.

The head of Christian's department had a Common Market face. He put his drink down on the Chopin and said, 'I don't really know you well enough to tell you this story.' Grace watched the room rippling in mirrored waters: such slow movement, such pastels; and, again, herself – upholstered, decorated, insured, and, for the first time, utterly alone. A big woman in violet leaned against the mantel, purpling the view. Christian's chief said, 'Now comes the bawdy part.' Grace listened abstractedly to the end of the joke. When she did not smile, Sir Manfred was displeased; and looked at her white flesh as if to say, You started it. He took up his drink and moved off toward the bookcase: 'I'm a voracious reader.' He had left a circular stain on a nocturne.

She saw, or knew, that Angus Dance had come back into the room. Making sure about some cheese puffs, she found him close to her, talking to a black-haired, blue-eyed girl who had come with the Dalrymples.

And why on earth not? A man like that could not possibly be leading a celibate life, abstinent in tribute to her own romantic fancies.

'Grace, I've got the info for you on the *Tirpitz*.'

It was their oldest friend, whom she at once wished dead.

'Don't say I ever let you down. A promise is a promise. Twelfth of November forty-four.'

Grace folded her hands before her. Sunk.

'Capsized at her moorings. We'd disabled her with midget subs the year before, but the RAF gave her the coo de grass in forty-four. Somewhere in the Arctic Circle, up in the Norwegian fjords. Don't ask me to pronounce the place; it's one of those names with dots over the top of it.'

Angus Dance was back to back with them, well within earshot.

'Damn fool Germans brought her well within our range, you see. Always be relied on for the stupid thing. Utterly gormless. Well, does that take care of everything?'

'I'm grateful, Ernie.'

Ernie spoke no German but could do a good accent at parties. 'Effer at your serffice.' He clicked his heels.

Angus Dance was fetching an ashtray for the Dalrymple girl. He had said, 'They sank.' For Grace and Ernie, it was 'We sank' – even the schoolgirl Grace had attacked the great battleship *Tirpitz* with all her nine-year-old might. Angus Dance was out of it, free from guilt or glory. For him, Ernie and Grace might as well have rioted on Mafeking night.

Grace revolved a cold glass between her palms. Ernie ran a proprietary finger along the black waist of the piano, in the same way Christian had done with the rim of her dress. 'She took a thousand men to the bottom with her.'

People were kissing her, one after the other: 'Dored it, dored it. Simply dored it.' Angus Dance left on a wave of departures, shaking hands.

When it was over, they brought the Spode out from a safe place. Someone had broken a goblet of cut crystal.

Jeremy remarked, 'You did say smash.'

Two calico cats were let out mewing from the

upstairs bathroom, but would not touch leftovers. Jeremy and Hugh put the chest back between the windows. Rupert, who was not allowed to lift, helped Christian count empty bottles: 'I liked Doctor Dance the best.'

I, too.

Christian half-turned his head to where Grace stood, and lightly winked. 'So we have a crush on Doctor Dance, do we?' He had assembled the bottles in a box. 'I liked him myself.'

Later still, winding his bedside clock, Christian asked, 'Why on earth was Ernie babbling on like that about the *Tirpitz*? Or was it the *Scharnhorst*?'

Grace was drawing the black dress over her head. 'I think it was the *Scharnhorst*.'

He could have called next day to thank for the party but did not, although the phone rang all morning and Christian's chief sent flowers.

'It was a success, then,' announced Jeremy, who was becoming worldly.

Grace was turning over the mail.

Christian said, 'I don't know when I've seen a finer bunch of marguerites.'

Mrs Thrale was now embarked on the well-known stages of love: the primary stage being simple, if infinite, longing. She might, in a single morning, see a dozen Dances in the streets. Then, high-strung to an impossible phone-bell whose electric drill reverberated in her soul, she constructed myths and legends from a doorway kiss; that was the secondary phase. Tertiary was the belief that all significance was of her own deranged contriving, and any reciprocity on the part of Angus Dance a fantasy. She had no revelation to make to him: he had even seen her best dress.

The trouble was the very abundance of her feelings sufficed for mutuality. So much loving-kindness also made it appear moral.

The phases mixed and alternated. If he came on Sunday, to the art show, she would know.

Grace lay awake, then slept uneasily.

Christian said, 'You're up so early these days.'

'It's that dog next door, barking at daybreak.'

Rupert cackled. 'Like a rooster.'

By now, Mrs Thrale had committed adultery in her heart many times.

On the Sunday, Christian took the boys to a horse show. Christian knew quite a bit about horses – their dimensions and markings and matings, their agilities. The boys, too, could adroitly use words like 'roan', 'Skewbald', and 'Gelding'.

'We should be back by six.'

Grace said, 'I might look in at the art show.'

When they had gone out she made up her face with care. She put on a heavy blue coat that was old but became her. It was a raw day, almost lightless; heavy clouds suggested snow. In a shop window she saw herself clasping her scarf together – hurrying, aglow.

A woman at the door charged her 10p. The floor of dirty wooden boards was uneven, and scrunched as she walked in. She was almost alone in the hall but could not bring herself to look about for Angus Dance. A fat man in a mackintosh stepped back to get perspective and collided: 'Sorry.' There were two or three elderly couples who had nothing else to do, and a dejected girl who was perhaps one of the exhibitors. The paint was in many cases green and red, in whorls; or had been applied thinly in angular greys. She knew he would not come.

When she left the place it was getting dark and there was sleet. She did not want to go home; it was as if her humiliation must be disclosed there. She shrank from home as from extra punishment – as a child, mauled by playmates, might fear parental scolding for torn clothes. But stumbled along with no other possibility. Pain rose up from her thorax, and descended like sleet behind her eyes. It was scarcely credible there should be no one to comfort her.

She thought: My mortification. And for the first time realized that the word meant death.

Alone at home, she went into the bathroom and leaned both hands on the sink, pondering. This anguish must be centred on some object other than Angus Dance. Such passion could scarcely have to do with him – the red-haired Doctor Dance of flesh and blood and three months' acquaintance – but must be fixed on a vision. This mirror, in its turn, showed her intent, exposed, breathing heavily. She had never seen herself so real, so rare.

She had just taken off her coat when they came in from the horse show, speaking in a practised manner of chestnuts and bays. Christian had been jostled in the Underground: 'Perhaps I'm not suited to the mass society.'

Grace said, 'Perhaps we are the mass society.'

Monday was Mrs Thrale's day for the hairdresser. She said, 'Mario, I have some grey hairs,' and put her hand to her brow. 'Here.' He took her head between his hands, under a light, as if it were a skull held *norma frontalis*. Alas, poor Grace. After a while he said, 'It is not a case for dyeing.'

He released her. 'You are not ready to dye.'

'No.'

'Being fair, you can wait a bit.' Grace sat in a plastic chair and he said, 'It is worse for the dark ladies.'

When she was settled under the dryer with *Vogue* and *The Gulag Archipelago*, the immemorial pathos of the place struck at her. There was hardly a young woman present, except the shampoo girl whose hipless jeans and prominent pectoral arch made Grace Thrale's soft flesh appear historic. Grace looked down at her own round little arms, stared at them as into a portrait by an Old Master. She thought of her body, which had never been truly slim, and showed a white mesh from bearing children, and now must passively await decay and mutilation. Her hands, clasped over a magazine picture of a bronze man on a beach, instinctively assumed an attitude of resignation. She read, 'The Aga Khan in a rare moment of relaxation.' But perceived herself in that instant entering into a huge suspense, lonely and universal.

That night Grace dreamed her own death.

The following morning she made an excuse to telephone the hospital.

'Doctor Dance has been off with a heavy cold.'

She said it was not important, and hung up. The bad cold arousing scorn, she said aloud, 'I would have got there,' meaning to the art show; which was perfectly true. She went upstairs and made the beds, and thought in derision: Scotsmen are scarcely Latin lovers.

Equilibrium did not last. On her way downstairs there was the same thoracic pain, a colossal suffering, grandiose, of a scale and distinction to which she, Grace Thrale of London W8 7EF, hardly seemed entitled. She sat in the kitchen and thought: I am overwrought; and perhaps am mad. Oh God, I must break myself of this.

Break, break, break. You said smash. A crush.

It occurred to her, in her isolation, that books might have helped. It was the first time she had reckoned with the fact she did not read, that neither she nor Christian read – and here was the true discovery, for she had relied on him to maintain a literary household. They had dozens of books, on shelves that took up half a wall; not to speak of the Penguins. And would send to the library regularly for the latest: she had the Iris Murdoch in the house, as well as the Solzhenitsyn. Voracious readers. But a state of receptiveness in which another's torment might reach into her own soul, through which her infatuation might be defined and celebrated – there was none of that. Christian confidently presented himself as a man of letters: 'I'm rereading Conrad this winter.' But *Within the Tides* had lain on his night table since December.

Christian came home and kissed her. 'I have spoken to those people about that yipping dog.'

'You haven't.'

'Certainly. You can't go sleepless for ever. They have agreed to keep the animal indoors.'

She wished he had not said 'the animal'.

He thumped his briefcase on to the hall table. 'And I actually used the word "yip".'

In her dream, Christian had been weeping.

Grace got up in the night and went downstairs. She took *Wuthering Heights* from a shelf and stood by the windows in the moonlight, keeping the ceaseless watch of her passion. She had no right to utter the name of Angus Dance, or to give him an endearment even in thought – never having done these things in life. She might as well have called on Heathcliff, or Aeneas. The book, an old edition, weighed in her hand. She knew she would not read it; but wondered if you might open at any page and find truth, like the Bible. She passed her other hand down her body, and thought her small feet irresistibly beautiful as they showed beneath her nightgown.

In the morning Christian said, 'Perhaps we need a new mattress.'

When the marguerites began to fester, Grace put them in the garbage. The card, still attached, said 'With Homage', and had an ink line through the surname. She swirled water in the vase and remembered: 'I didn't laugh at his off-colour joke.'

Christian was worried, but said, 'You certainly don't have to take insults to further my career': to forestall her thoughts. After a moment he asked, 'What was the joke anyway?'

'I couldn't for the life of me work it out.' They both burst out laughing. No reply could have pleased him more. Perfect, sheltered Grace. Once, during a holiday on Corsica, he had turned her face away from the spectacle, as he called it, of a fistfight.

Late that day she met Angus Dance in the street. She had bought narcissus to replace the daisies, and stood holding them downward in her hand. She could think of nothing to say that would equal the magical silent discourse of her reverie.

He said, 'Are you all right?'

'I haven't been sleeping properly.' She might as well have said, I love you. 'Except with pills.'

'What are you taking?' For a moment authority passed back to him.

They then spoke of his heavy cold. And she would bring Rupert in for a check-up at the end of the month. Despite sleeplessness, her skin glowed like his own.

He said, 'Do you have time for a coffee?'

So Grace Thrale sat at a Formica table and Angus Dance hung his flannel jacket on a peg. He wore a pale woollen waistcoat knitted by his mother. His hair in itself was enough to attract attention: his northern light, his blaze of midnight sun. They scarcely spoke, though leaning forward from a delicate readiness, until the girl came to take their order. Both his accent and an oddly aspirated *r* were more pronounced. Grace thought her own speech indistinct, and made an effort to talk out.

'I have been wondering how you were.' All things considered, the boldest remark she had ever made. She was surprised by her definite voice, her firm hand efficiently taking sugar, when the whole of Creation, the very texture of the firmament, was wrought, receptive, cream-coloured, like his sweater.

He said he ought to go to Burnham-on-Crouch to see about his boat, which was up on the slips for scraping and red lead. Some recaulking was also needed. 'I don't feel up to it, somehow.' The commonplaces, the withholdings, were a realisation in themselves. Her scented flowers stood between them in a tumbler of water, pent within a green string. 'I'm not much of a sailor – the genuine ones are fanatical. I took it up after a bad experience. I suppose it was a means of motion when everything was standing still.'

'Was it when your marriage broke up?'

'No. This was a later repudiation.' He smiled. 'I don't know that any of this can be very interesting. Such usual griefs.'

'To me they are not usual.' She could not imagine Christian, for whom acceptance was imperative, recounting his rebuffs, or acknowledging 'my griefs'. Even in the entrancement of the coffee-shop the threat came over her that Christian was in this the more infirm, the more defenceless; and that Angus Dance was fortified by reversals, and by his refusal to dissimulate. She recalled his simple commitment to Rupert, how he had said, 'I promise.' Such fearlessness could not be required of Christian.

When she made contrasts to Christian it was not just the disloyalty but that Christian always seemed to gain.

Doctor Dance offered buns. 'I had a grand time at your party. I should have called to say so.'

Grace thought of the scuttling of the *Tirpitz*, and the chief's commemorative flowers, a soaked wreath on swirling waters. Lest we forget. 'It seems so long ago.'

'I've not seen you since.'

It was the mingling of great and trivial that could not be misunderstood.

He went on, 'Yet we are so close.'

She fell silent, leaning back into colours and shadows of the room: not in fulfilment, which could hardly be, but in voluptuous calm, at peace. Her hand was outstretched on the table, the sleeve pushed up. It was the first time he had seen her inner arm. She knew it might be the only such passage between them, ever. If the usual griefs were coming to her at last, so was this unprecedented perfection.

Grace was seated at the piano. She turned a sheet of music, but did not play. Rupert came and stood beside her. 'What is it?'

'It's Scarlatti.'

He had meant, What's wrong?

Like a lover, he stood near enough to suggest she should embrace him. With her right arm she drew him against her side. Her left hand rested on the keys. She leaned her head to his upper arm. It was like an Edwardian photograph. She said, 'I do love you, Rupey.' This was the last child with whom she could get away with such a thing – and only then because his illness had given them an extension during which a lot might be overlooked. They both knew it. Emulating her mood, the boy became pensive, languid; and at the same time remained omnipotent.

She said again, 'I do.' To get him to say it back. She thought: So now it has come round: *I* am trying to draw strength from *them*. She thought the word 'adulteress', and it was archaic as being stoned to death – a bigoted word like 'Negress' or 'Jewess' or 'seamstress' or 'poetess'; but precise.

Her left hand sounded notes in the bass: sombre, separate, instructed. The room received them dispassionately. There was a click of her ring on ivory. She rocked the boy a little with her arm, and could feel the plaster armouring his X-rayed ribs. She took her hand from the piano and put both arms about him, her fingers locked over his side, her breast and brow turned to his body. This was less like a photograph.

He said, 'What's up, Mum?' Moving his imprisoned arm, he put his own hand to the treble and struck a discordant series of keys, stressing and repeating vehement high notes. She released him, but he jarred a few last perplexed excited sounds; and stood, still touching her, swayed between childhood and sensuality.

Christian came in with papers in his hand. 'What's this, a duet?'

The boy sauntered off and switched on the telly. The News flickered over jagged devastations – Beirut or Belfast, the Bronx or Bombay.

Christian said, 'Grace, I must speak to you.'

Rupert yelled, 'It's a programme on Pompeii.'

Grace sat with Christian on a sofa that was rarely used because of the velvet. He told her, 'Something momentous has occurred.'

In her mind, Grace Thrale swooned.

'I have been given Africa.'

He might have been Alexander, or Antony. The younger Scipio. Grace stared whitely, and he added, 'South of the Sahara.'

She was looking through such tears as would never rise for Angus Dance, who could not need, or evoke, pity for impercipience or self-exposure. She wept for Christian, insulated in the non-conducting vainglory of his days, and might then have told him all, out of sheer fidelity to the meaning of things. She said, 'My darling.'

'There's nothing in the world to cry about.' Christian touched her face, pleased. 'I can assure you.' Perfect Grace. He unrolled the departmental chart in his hand. A small box at the top of the page littered into larger boxes underneath, fathering endless enclosures of self-esteem. He pointed – here, and here. 'Talbot-Sims will only be Acting. But for me it's the real thing.' As he leaned to show the pedigree, there was a sparse, greying place on top of his sandy head. He said, 'My youth was against me,' brushing a speck from the flawless page. 'But in the end they waived seniority.' The chart started to curl at the edges, struggling to rescroll. 'It will make a whopping difference in the pension.'

Grace wondered if their severance from each other's thoughts and purposes had at any time appeared so conclusive to him; if ever she herself had so grossly disregarded. She wondered whether, during summer separations, or the time she went to Guernsey, he had perhaps loved, or slept with – the one need not preclude the other – someone else. It was hard to imagine him sufficiently headstrong for it, now he did not have the self-reliance to read a book. If he had loved another woman, Grace of all people would understand it. Magnanimity shaped a sad and vast perspective. Or it was merely a plea for leniency in her own case.

Christian put his arm around her, stooping from heights where officials waved seniority. 'I'm afraid we'll have to call off the Costa Brava. But when I've got things in hand I'll take you somewhere quiet.' His mind ranged, like the News, over ravaged nations, seeking a possibility. All was pandemonium – Portugal, Palestine, Tibet: called off, one after one. Elation weirdly faltered in his throat, as on a sob; but recklessly resumed: 'So you brought me luck, telling the old bastard off about his joke.'

Angus Dance came into the brick passage as the rain began. He started to run; at the same moment that Grace Thrale, entering from the opposite end, ran, too, under the rain.

Had it been possible to observe their meeting from above or alongside, like a sequence on film they would have been seen at first precipitate, heads lowered against weather; then slowed in realisation; and finally arrested. The arrestation being itself some peak of impetus, a consummation. They were then facing, about a yard apart, and rain was falling on Dance's hair and, like gauze, on Grace's coat of calamine blue. Ignored, the heavy rain was a cosmic attestation, more conclusive than an embrace.

Anyone seeing them would have said lovers.

Rain was silvering Dance's eyelids. He had taken hold of himself by the coat lapel. His expression was disarmed, pure with crisis. 'This is what I meant about being close.'

'Yes.'

'Shall we get to shelter?' As if they had not already got to shelter.

Sloshing along the narrow tunnel, he took her arm at last. By not embracing they had earned some such indulgence. They then stood under an awning at the exit of a supermarket; and he said, proving her more right than she had ever been about anything, 'You know that I love you.' It was the response she had not been able to compel from her own child.

She would not even brush the water from her hair or coat; and perhaps need never consider her appearance again. After moments during which the rain continued and they were nudged by shopping-bags, she said, 'It makes me happy.' She thought she would tell the simple truth, now that she was indomitable.

Opposite, there was the new hotel that took groups. Dance said, 'It would be a place to talk.'

'We can cross when it lets up.' Her self-possession surprised, as in the tea-shop.

He hesitated; and decided. 'Yes. I'll have to telephone about the appointments.'

She did not urge him to keep them. Nor did he ask if she was due in the Crescent. When the sky lightened, they crossed.

As they came into the hotel, the man at the desk put down the phone, saying 'Christ.' A heap of baggage – suitcases, golf-bags, holdalls in nylon plaid – was piled by the foot of the stairs. In the lounge, which was one floor up, they might already have been at an airport, waiting to depart. Pylons of the building were thinly encased in plastic wood, with little counters around them for ash trays or drinks. The sofas were hard and bright, yet far from cheerful. Slack curtains were tawdry with metallic threads, and on one wall there was a tessellated decoration of a cornucopia greenly disgorging.

As they entered, a group of women in trouser-suits got up to leave. An old man with an airline bag said, near tears, 'But they only had it in beige.'

Grace Thrale sat near a window, and Angus Dance went to telephone. Had it not been for him, how easily she might have fitted in here. The enclosure, nearly empty, enjoined subservience – was blank with the wrath, bewilderment, and touching faith of its usual aggregations. It was no use now trying this on Grace, who scarcely saw and was past condescending. With detachment that was another face of passion, she wondered in what circumstances she would leave this place and if she would ever go home. Abandoned by her, the house in the Crescent was worse than derelict, the life in it extinct: the roast attaining room temperature on the kitchen counter, an unfinished note to Grace's sister announcing Christian's promotion, a rock album that was a surprise for Hugh; and *Within the Tides*, unopened on the bedside table. All suspended, silent, enigmatical – slight things that might have dressed the cabins of the *Mary Celeste* or embellished a programme on Pompeii; trifles made portentous by rejection.

She got up and spread the two damp coats on a nearby seat, to deter. She stood at a concrete embrasure looking at the rain, and knew he had come back.

He sat beside her on hard red plastic and said, 'There's nothing to be afraid of.' He touched his fingers to hers, as once at the hospital. 'I am going away.' You could see the colour ebbing down through clear lit levels of his skin. 'I have been offered a position in Leeds.'

She sat with the air of supremacy, the triumphant bearing summoned for a different outcome. When she did not speak, he went on, 'You must not think I would ever try to damage your life.' Her life, which she stood ready to relinquish: whose emblems she had been coolly dispersing, as she might have picked off the dead heads of flowers.

He said, 'As if I would seek to injure you.'

As if she would not have gone up with him to a room in this place and made love, if he had wished it.

He was making an honest woman of her. She deserved no credit from the beneficiaries, having already thrown them over: love would be concealed, like unworthiness, from them, from him. When she had coveted his standards, she had naïvely imagined them compatible with her passion. It was another self-revelation – that she should have assumed virtue could be had so quickly, and by such an easy access as love. It was hard to tell, in all this, where her innocence left off and guilt began.

Scrutinising Angus Dance's drained face and darkened eyes, his mouth not quite controlled, Grace Thrale was a navigator who seeks land in a horizon deceitful with vapours. Eventually she asked, repeating her long lesson, 'Is this a promotion?'

'An advancement, yes.'

Such conquerors, with their spoils, their cities and continents – Leeds, Africa. Advancing, progressing, all on the move: a means of motion. Only Grace was stationary, becalmed.

'In that way, also, it's necessary. I can't go on doing the present job for ever.'

Only Grace might go on doing for ever. Might look up Leeds in the phone book, like Dorset. Realisation was a low protracted keening in her soul. Here at last was her own shipwreck – a foundering beyond her parents' capsized ferry. She might have howled, but said instead what she had heard in plays: 'Of course there would have been no future to this.'

Colour came back on his cheeks like blood into contusions. He got up quickly and, as if they were in a private room, stood by the concrete window; then leaned against a column, facing her, his arms spread along the ridge meant for ash-trays, his durable body making a better architecture, a telamon. 'A man should have past and present as well as future.' He moved his hand emphatically, and a dish of peanuts spilled in silence: it was a gesture that laid waste, as if a fragment of the column disintegrated. 'Do you not think I see it constantly, the dying who've not lived? It is what we are being, not what we are to be. Rather, they are the same thing.'

'I know that.' Even her children were already staked on the future – their aptitudes for science or languages, what did they want to be, to be; they had never been sincerely asked what they would be now. She said, 'Even those who have truly lived will die. It is hard to say which is the greater irony.' Such discoveries were owed to him. She rose to his occasion, and no doubt would soon sink back, incurious; would go, literally, into a decline.

He said, 'I am near thirty-three years of age, and live with too much vacancy.' She saw his rectitude existing in a cleared space like his parents' uncluttered house. He told her, 'You cannot imagine – well, I do not mean that unkindly. But you with your completeness – love, children, beauty, troops of friends – how would you understand such formlessness as mine? How would you know solitude, or despair?'

They were matters she had glimpsed in a mirror. She felt his view of her existence settling on her like an ornate, enfeebling garment; closing on her like a trap. She leaned back on the unyielding sofa, and he stood confronting. It was an allegorical contrast – sacred and profane love: her rapture offered like profanity. To assert, or retrieve, she said, 'Yet there has been nothing lovelier in my life than the times we sat together at the hospital and looked at the photographs.'

He came back to the sofa and replaced his hand on hers – a contact both essential and external, like the print of fingers on X-rays. 'It was like Paolo and Francesca.'

She would have to look it up when she got home. But stared at his hand on hers and thought, without mockery: Scarcely Latin lovers.

He said, 'It's true we could not have stood the lies.'

The first lie was Grace drawing off her dress, her head shrouded in black, her muffled voice saying, '*Scharnhorst*.' She said, 'In my married life I never so much as exchanged an unchaste kiss, until with you on my birthday.'

He smiled. Perfect sheltered Grace. 'There is so little laughter in illicit love. Whatever the theme, there must always be the sensation of laughing at someone else's expense.'

Grace had last laughed with Christian, over Sir Manfred's joke. She said, 'I am serious.' The kiss, the lie, the laughter – nothing would be serious again by that measurement. 'I am serious,' she said, as he smiled from his greater experience and lesser insight; as he looked with the wrong solicitude. Grace would not be called upon to testify. She remembered how, on tumultuous Corsica, her head had been turned away.

'In a new place', she supposed, 'you will get over this.'

'I still dream about a girl I knew when I was eighteen.' He would not conform with her platitudes; he would not perceive her truth. He would dream of Grace, in Leeds. He said, 'Memories cool to different temperatures at different speeds.' He glanced about, at the figured rug and tinselled curtains, the column splintered into peanuts, the drab cornucopia: 'What an awful place.' And his condemnation was the prelude to farewell.

Grace Thrale said, 'It is the world.'

'I've said many things to you in thought, but they were never hopeless like this. Nor did they take place in any material world.' He then corrected himself. 'Of course there has been desire,' dismissing this extravagance. His accent intruded, and he allowed time for speech to recover itself, mastering language like tears. 'What I mean is, in thoughts one keeps a reserve of hope, in spite of everything. You cannot say goodbye in imagination. That is something you can only do in actuality, in the flesh. Even desire has less to do with the flesh than goodbye.'

His face had never appeared less contemporary. Was one of those early photographs, individual with suffering and conscience.

'So I am to lose you.' She might have been farewelling a guest: Dored it, dored it. Dored you.

He said, 'I cannot do any more,' and withdrew his refractive touch and passed his hand through his bright hair as in some ordinary bafflement. He got up again and took his coat from the chair, and stood over her. All these actions, being performed very rapidly, reminded that he was expert in contending with pain. 'I'll drop you. I'm taking a taxi.' His reversion to daily phrases was deathly. It was ultimate proof that men were strong, or weak.

They stood up facing, as if opposed; and onlookers were relieved to see them normal.

'I'll stay on here a few minutes.' She could not contemplate the taxi in which he resolutely would not embrace her. She clasped her hands before her in the composed gesture with which she sometimes enfolded desperation; raising her head to his departure, she was a wayside child who salutes a speeding car on a country road.

When Grace came down into the street, the rain had stopped and the darkness arrived. Men and women were coming from their work, exhausted or exhilarated, all pale. And the wet road shone with headlamps, brighter than the clear black sky with stars. Engines, voices, footsteps, and a transistor or two created their geophysical tremor of a world in motion. This show of resumption urged her, gratuitously, toward the victors – to Jeremy whose eye needed bathing with boric acid, and Hugh's bent for mathematics, and Rupert's unexpected interest in Yeats, and Christian saying 'This is the best lamb in years.' All of that must riot in triumph over her, as she would find out soon enough. They would laugh last, with the innocent appalling laughter of their rightful claim and licit love.

With these prospects and impressions, Grace Marian Thrale, forty-one years old, stood silent in a hotel doorway in her worn blue coat and looked at the cars and the stars, with the roar of existence in her ears. And, like any great poet or tragic sovereign of antiquity, cried on her Creator and wondered how long she must remain on such an earth.

The Misfortunes of Ambrose Gwinnett

RAYNER HEPPENSTALL

IF THIS were a play, the curtain would first rise on an inn parlour. As we are in the reign of Queen Anne, the dressing of the stage would suggest this fact as far as it might. As we are close to the sea, that fact also might be suggested. An East Indiaman anchored in the Downs might even be visible through the window, once the blind was raised, for it is quite early in the morning, and the blinds may not have been raised when our principal character comes in through the door and stands looking about.

He is a gentlemanly young man of twenty-one, not quite at his best. Mrs Sawyer comes bustling in, perhaps raising the blinds, and then sees him. With a glad cry, she says, 'Ambrose!' and rushes to embrace him. He is less effusive, but very glad to see her, she being the older sister whom he has walked all the way from Canterbury to see.

But how is it he has arrived so early in the day? He explains.

'The road was full of men and horses coming from the Michaelmas fair, and I am not accustomed to long walking. Besides, I had a colic. I got to Deal and felt I could go no farther. The inns were full with officers and sailors from ships in the Downs. At last, I reached the New Inn, and the landlady there –'

'Anne Collins. She and I are great friends. We have done each other many a favour.'

'– said I could sleep on a chair in her parlour. She said you and she were friends and had done each other many a favour.'

If this were rather a novel than a play, we should perhaps have started farther back, with Ambrose Gwinnett's arrival at the New Inn, in Deal, or farther back still, with his departure from Canterbury, where his father had a trade in seamen's slops at the sign of the Blue Anchor and he, articled these five years to George Roberts, attorney (being a well-schooled youth), had received permission from his master to visit his sister, Vanessa Sawyer, near Deal. In a play, these facts would be awkward to put across, since they (the name and trade of Ambrose's master, and the trade and place of business of their father) were known to Mrs Sawyer, but a bit of asking after this person and that might get them across. There would be no difficulty about the incidents of the night, which make a tale anybody might very well tell his sister.

He would tell how the landlady of the New Inn had taken him into the parlour. On the chair where Ambrose was to sleep sat a man in nightgown and cap, by a dying fire, counting money. This was the landlady's uncle by marriage, Richard Collins. He was boatswain of an East Indiaman then at anchor in the Downs. It would be better if he shared his double bed with the newcomer. This he reluctantly agreed to do.

He put his money in a money-belt, strapped this about him and took up a candle. The two men went up to bed.

They had not been long abed when Ambrose Gwinnett's colic began to trouble him. He awoke his bedfellow and asked the way to the privy. This was, of course, in the garden. The string which lifted the sneck was broken, said Collins, and you needed a knife to lift it. If the young man felt in the right-hand pocket of Collins's trousers, he would find a penknife which he could use.

Gwinnett found the knife and, making as little noise as possible, set out in the dark for the garden and the privy. When he opened the penknife, a coin dropped out of the handle. This he put in his pocket and without difficulty raised the sneck and opened the privy door. His bowels were very troublesome, and he stayed quite a long time on the privy seat.

When he returned to the room in which he had been sharing a bed with Richard Collins, he felt around for the trousers, but they had gone. So had Collins. Gwinnett got back into his side of the bed and dozed uneasily until first light, the sun being up at about seven o'clock. Then he arose, dressed and went downstairs. The landlady got up, half-dressed. He paid his reckoning and was instructed on the road to take to his sister's – a distance of three miles, along the coast, we shall suppose, to Kingsdown.

Here, for the purposes of a play, we should somewhat have to invent; for, while Ambrose himself might well forget to mention such details, we must suppose that his sister would ask him what account he had given Anne Collins of the disappearance of her uncle and whether he had given her the penknife and the coin. It seems likely that he had said nothing about these matters, feeling perhaps very poorly and thinking of nothing but how to get to his sister's.

There seems enough good reason to suppose that the Sawyers' hostelry was at Kingsdown. We can only guess whether it was the Zetland Arms or the Rising Sun or on the site which either of these would come to occupy. On the whole, the Rising Sun seems the likelier, because that bit farther inland, the Zetland Arms being so much out on the beach that a boy would hardly be driving cows home to be milked at it. However, here we anticipate.

We must suppose that at some point towards the end of Ambrose Gwinnett's narration his brother-in-law, Tom Sawyer, would enter. He, too, had been a seafaring man, latterly serving with a privateer in the late French war, so that it was with prize money he had bought the inn and married the daughter of a trader in seamen's slops in Canterbury. He would know whether the level of a spring tide had in the night joined with a fair wind to hasten the departure of an East Indiaman and so accounted for the abrupt departure of her boatswain, Richard Collins, from the New Inn.

He perhaps showed Ambrose to his room, while Vanessa made their breakfast, with uncustomed coffee and the finest Jamaica sugar. It may be that, after his unrestful night, Ambrose went up to bed and slept for a while.

So long as this is a play, we have no means of knowing what was happening meanwhile at the New Inn in Deal. Let us keep it that way, for the moment. What we are next aware of is galloping hoofs approaching, whether on a record or imitated with at least two and preferably three pairs of cleverly manipulated half coconut-shells (when these have come up to full volume they must not, of course, abruptly stop, for the horses would still do a little stamping about outside the Sawyers' inn, until such time as we hear them gallop off again). An officer of the law enters and demands Ambrose Gwinnett, who is wanted on charges of robbery and murder committed last night at or near the New Inn, Deal.

It might, indeed, be better if he were off stage at the moment, for then the officer (or two officers) of the law, instead of simply identifying him and constituting him the King's prisoner, might tell Sawyer, who was a respected man and probably known to him (them), as much of the discovered circumstances as we need to know. The chief of these was that Mrs Collins had found the sheets on her double bed stained with blood and that a trail of blood led downstairs and out of the house all the way to last night's high-water mark of the sea.

His sister now coming down with Ambrose

Gwinnett, the officer or the senior of the two would no doubt ask him if that were his name and ask him whether he had spent last night or part of it at the New Inn, Deal. He might also make him turn his pockets out, and exclaim with triumph at the penknife and at a coin which was a William and Mary guinea and which Mrs Collins had specially mentioned. The initials 'RC' had been scratched on it. Of the money-belt there appeared to be no trace, nor had Gwinnett an excess of money on him. For the fact that such an excess had not been entrusted to his keeping Sawyer's word would be accepted.

When it was announced to him that he was the King's prisoner, some form of gyves or manacles would be fastened to Ambrose Gwinnett's wrists (we cannot call them handcuffs, for that word was not to come into use for sixty-six years more, the date at present being 1709). And out they would go to the man who was holding the horses and gallop off, while the Sawyers speculated in silent dismay or with tears and a good curtain-line, if one occurs to us.

I ought, that is certain, to have made up my mind whether I wanted to write a play or a novel. The fact is that I would have liked to write a play, but foresee difficulties which I do not think I could surmount to my own satisfaction. It will be in the last act that these become, if not precisely insurmountable, yet surmountable only with the aid of too much invention, not all of it plausible.

The first scene of the first act (for that is what it would have to be, not a whole act) goes, I think, like a dream, as I first planned it. The few little difficulties I mentioned would require only elementary stagecraft to surmount them. The second and longer scene would be just as easy and natural but for considerations affecting the relation of real to stage time, though we are helped in this by the weather.

The scene is unchanged. The time which has elapsed need not be great, in view of how little delay there generally was in those days in the proceedings of *oyer* and *terminer* and general gaol delivery, there being no prisons in which long sentences could properly be served and no more than the sketchiest provision outside London for protracted remand.

We may perhaps here speculate a little more than we could do on the stage about proceedings in the case of Ambrose Gwinnett. He was, we know, taken to Maidstone gaol, and it would be at assizes in Maidstone for the county of Kent that he came up for trial. We have, unfortunately, no record either of the public hearing or of the evidence against him, which must have been taken before magistrates who in those days acted more like French *juges d'instruction* than magistrates in England and Wales or in Scotland do now. For, even then, justice was not quite such a rough-and-ready business as we may think. To convict him had required more than the shrill accusations of an innkeeper's wife and the eager compliance of her neighbours.

Hers would, it is true, be the chief evidence for the prosecution at Ambrose's trial, hers and that of whoever came forward to say that he had traced a trail of drops of blood from the New Inn to the water's edge, but perhaps that had been a zealous officer of the law. George Roberts or counsel bespoken by him cannot have insisted strongly enough on what was certainly a point of law: that no *corpus delicti* had been found on either count – no actual body on the count of murder; no proceeds of theft on that of robbery, or at most a penknife and a single William and Mary guinea, for which the accused had offered a plausible explanation. No experienced luggerman was brought from Deal to Maidstone to say what the tides would have done with a body pushed into the water at that point.

The circumstantial evidence, however little embroidered, was strong, especially that of the bloody bed. An advertisement in the *London Gazette* had not brought a live Richard Collins forward. It did not appear that he had joined his ship. And so, inspired if not bullied by what judge we do not know, a Maidstone jury had brought in its verdict: that Ambrose Gwinnett had murdered Richard Collins and stolen his money, afterwards pushing his body into the sea, where it had vanished. Sentence was passed: that he was to be taken to Deal and hanged near the scene of his crime, to be afterwards hung in what were called chains outside the town.

From Maidstone to Deal the distance is forty miles. If Gwinnett were trundled the whole way by cart (the halter tied round his arms, so that he could not move these), he cannot, that Wednesday, leaving Maidstone at six o'clock in the morning, have been in Deal until fairly late in the afternoon. It was a stormy day, the wind and rain so violent that the sheriff and his officers, soaked to the skin, could barely sit their horses. The hangman, we may imagine, did his job hastily and left the body hanging less than the customary half-hour (it was sometimes an hour), then cut it down and dumped it in the New Inn to be prepared for gibbeting. This meant wrapping it in tarred calico and fastening up the parcel with iron bands. Then it was taken some way south of the town to the gibbet erected in a common field and hoisted up to a swivel, to which it was riveted, carelessly no doubt.

Tom Sawyer has been to witness the execution of his brother-in-law and stayed to see part of the business of his gibbeting on land adjoining the northernmost of his own meadows. Vanessa Sawyer, *née* Gwinnett, stayed behind at the inn, not purely out of delicacy of feeling, but because somebody had to be there. Officers from a privateer are staying at the inn. They will not be sailing that night, because of the weather. On the other hand, they may have to go on board, for there is quite a sea even in the Downs. Instructions relative to these facts and the bestowal of their baggage and what they will be requiring in the way of food and service will have to be given, and it is likely enough that one of the officers will have felt a need to express sympathy with a landlady known to be under a strain.

We do not know just what time of day or season of the year it is, but daylight will be fading. What effects of the day's weather are apparent in the inn parlour – in the way, for instance, of plants seen blowing outside or rain beating on the window – must be left to the director. When Tom Sawyer enters they must be conspicuous.

We, the audience, are still in ignorance of all that has happened, even of the fact that Ambrose Gwinnett has been tried and convicted at Maidstone, let alone of his hanging at Deal and gibbeting nearer this way that afternoon. This has to be established in the dialogue between husband and wife. It ought not to be difficult, though how affecting it is will depend on the playwright.

A boy enters. He has just driven cows in from the far field for milking. He still carries a stick and is dishevelled. He places his muddy feet carefully, but knows that he will be forgiven for bursting in like this when the innkeeper and his wife have heard what he has to say. This is that the body on the gibbet is alive. He heard it groan. Also, the calico has come loose from the face, and the eyes are open otherwise than in a lifeless stare.

Sawyer is out of the house with all speed. His wife is about to follow him, but thinks again. The boy follows. Night is coming on. Taking a brand from the fire, she lights candles and then a lamp. Outside the house, Sawyer is heard calling to the boy to bring an axe, a saw, a ladder. Mrs Sawyer fetches her cloak, a bonnet and pattens, but again thinks twice and puts them down. A privateer officer comes in and enquires what is amiss. Told, he further enquires in what direction he must go to help Sawyer. He calls a fellow-officer, and they go.

Unless we black out the stage for a while, it will be necessary here to pass a fair amount of time with hithering and thithering of neighbours and inn servants, for it appears that there was no way of getting the body down but by cutting down the gibbet or uprooting it. Eventually, the body is brought in and put into a warm bed, and a barber surgeon comes to blood it. It is now that the problem arises of how to get Ambrose Gwinnett away from the inn before the destruction of the gibbet is discovered. The answer lies with the privateer's officers. They will take him out to their ship, where a literate young man would be useful in keeping the steward's accounts.

To invent business here should not be hard. The hanged man may already be able to walk, supported. If not, he will have to be carried down to a boat. It is a rough night, but from a window of the inn the women should be able to see the men with their lanterns go with Ambrose to the boat and this push off, perhaps obscurely see it rowed all the way to the ship, the wind being westerly and off shore.

I see that I have given very little space to this scene, though to my mind it would be considerably longer than the preceding. A great deal of dialogue would need to be invented, but on the other hand its general purport seems to me to be always clear. The small parts (I have merely indicated inn servants and neighbours) would have to be distinct. There would perhaps be a cowman, an old woman who might be the mother of one of the Sawyers, a bustling and officious neighbour, a gaping idiot. Their various reactions to what, let's face it, is an unusual situation could, I feel sure, be made interesting. As to the body of a hanged man, the state in which it is brought in could hardly fail to have some shock value. The iron bands could not have been fully removed outside, and the tarred calico would have to be unwrapped. This is perhaps a matter rather for the director than the playwright, who would nevertheless have to write the lines needed.

At the beginning of Act Two it will occasion surprise that the language being spoken on the stage is no longer English. There will be members of the audience who identify it as Spanish. The next shock will lie in perceiving that one of the speakers is Ambrose Gwinnett, some four or five years older than when we last saw him.

The place is Havana, a city some two hundred years old and with a population of not less than twenty thousand. Built of coral limestone like all the main buildings and churches of the city, the gaol is on the Prado. The curtain rises on the gaoler's room. Ambrose Gwinnett is seated at a table, with papers and an inkwell in front of him. Beside him stands the gaoler, before him a prisoner with a warder. The prisoner's hands are tied behind his back. Gwinnett intimates to the gaoler that he has finished with this man. The gaoler tells the warder to remove him. This the warder does. As he is leaving, the gaoler asks the warder how many more there are. The warder says that the next will be the last. The gaoler tells him to bring the man in straight away.

The last of the prisoners comes in and is positioned in front of Gwinnett, who addresses him in English. The man looks searchingly at Gwinnett. He says that his name is Richard Collins. Gwinnett does not at first react to this information. The man says that he was pressed on board the ship and that he served unwillingly. Gwinnett begins to look searchingly at him. He reads the name he has written down and echoes it.

'Were you ever in Deal?' he asks.

'I was pressed in Deal,' says the man.

'How many years ago?'

'Four, five.'

'Then I was hanged and gibbeted on your account.'

The two gaze incredulously at each other.

'You came to the New Inn,' says Collins, 'and my niece....'

Gwinnett's story we know. Collins's is that he had been blooded that day and that, while Gwinnett was out attending to his colic, the wound had opened and that he had left his bed and gone out to knock up the surgeon. In the street, he had been seized by a press-gang, dragged (the surgeon's cut still bleeding) to a boat at the sea's edge and conveyed aboard a privateer in the Downs, which had presently sailed. His wound attended to by the ship's surgeon, he had been compelled to serve on board the privateer, which in truth was no better than a pirate ship, until, in desperate conflict with a Spanish man-of-war off Yucatan, their crew had been reduced to nine hands, who had been brought into the harbour of Havana that morning.

Gwinnett's ship, which had been an honest privateer, had not fought so hard, and with him forty crew-members had landed and been interned. That had been four years ago. But the gaoler is fidgeted by this long exchange in a language he does not understand. Gwinnett apologises in Spanish. He knows this prisoner, he says in the same language, and will answer for him. May his hands be untied? This is done. The gaoler and the warder go.

After three years, Gwinnett continues in English, Spain and Britain being then momentarily at peace, the captives were to be put on board transports and shipped to Pennsylvania. It would not have suited Gwinnett to return to English jurisdiction, despite the having been hanged once. He solicited the head gaoler to allow him to remain, and the governor of the island was persuaded that an employee who knew both English and Spanish and was a lawyer's clerk into the bargain would be very useful in dealing with British and American pirates.

As far as English law was concerned, the two men could now very well go home together, and Gwinnett would be pardoned. The governor of the island would no doubt be sorry to see him go, but he was no longer a prisoner. The governor was a fair-minded man and would probably, for Gwinnett's sake, accept Collins's plea that only *force majeure* had impelled him into courses of piracy.

The chain of coincidence was not yet broken. It is to be supposed that Richard Collins boarded the right ship, but this time, walking along the Cuban shore at night in the wrong direction, Ambrose Gwinnett fell in with pirates, who impressed him into service.

Their captain was Brian Walsh, an Irishman. He befriended Gwinnett and made him purser, in charge of enormous riches stowed on the pirates' centre of operations, Swallow Island, twelve leagues inside the Gulf of Mexico. Gwinnett was later to describe Walsh as a most execrable and bloody villain. This was ungrateful. After capturing a Jamaican ship loaded with a cargo of sugar and rum, Walsh drank himself to death, leaving a will which made Gwinnett sole heir to a fortune of forty thousand pounds sterling, which would make him almost a millionaire today. As he now owned the ship as well, Gwinnett appointed the first mate captain and ordered him to make for Port Royal, it being his intention that in Jamaica his crew should abandon their piratical ways and settle down.

On the voyage from Swallow Island, however, their ship went down, with all its treasure. Those who remained afloat in the ship's boats included Ambrose Gwinnett, but the others threw him overboard, perhaps understandably. Once again he was lucky in that a Spanish ship picked him up, but unlucky in that the Spaniards decided that he was a pirate. They were right, of course, unless he had meant, on arrival in Jamaica, to disgorge all Brian Walsh's ill-gotten gains, which he was never to claim that he had intended to do. As to the men in the boats, they had probably suspected all along that there was something fishy about Brian Walsh's will, as there probably was. We can hardly suppose that, after so many years, Ambrose would remain quite the spotless child of misfortune we first met.

The Spaniards sentenced him to serve in their Mediterranean galleys, which he did for two years. Then, in an engagement with an Algerian *chebek*, he suffered a real misfortune. He lost a leg. He was to say that, in consequence of this loss, he escaped from the Spaniards, but that seems unlikely. The fact of the matter is that a galley-slave with one leg is not of much use. Perhaps he was encouraged to escape. At any rate, he arrived back in England to find all his relations dead. Richard Collins had not reached home.

The date is said to have been 1730. The years accounted for since 1709 are a long way short of twenty-one. The likeliest guess is that twelve or so had been spent with Brian Walsh.

By some such procedures as Paul Claudel employed in *Le Soulier de satin* and *Christophe Columb*, it might be possible to present on a stage years of miscellaneous adventure in the Caribbean and the Mediterranean. But I began by envisaging a straightforward comedy in three acts. This could still be managed if, on his return to England, Ambrose Gwinnett found a natural hearer for the account of his intervenient adventures.

His lack of a leg presents difficulties to the actor playing him, though such difficulties have been overcome with varying success in the past. But the awkwardness lies in finding him a proper interlocutor.

It may be assumed that he landed in Deal, for all ships bound for London lay up, however briefly, in the Downs, and he would certainly take a boat off to call on his sister and her husband at their inn. He would find new people there. His next call would very likely be the New Inn, where he would want to know if Richard Collins had appeared. He had not. He might there try to convince Anne Collins that he had met Richard Collins, her uncle, in the West Indies and had seen him off back to England; but, as he had never appeared, she would not believe him. Much as she might pity him for his leglessness, he would still be to her her uncle's murderer.

This is, in fact, the encounter which promises best for stage presentation. Another would be with Gwinnett's former master, the attorney, George Roberts, in Canterbury, if he were still alive. Either encounter would provide Gwinnett with an opportunity to recount his later adventures, but we should still require a last scene showing what finally became of him.

He ended up a roadsweeper, who from 1734 onwards swept the way between Mews Gate and Spring Gardens, Charing Cross. There is a broadsheet which contains his purported autobiography. The copy in the British Library is a second edition of 1770. On it, somebody has written, 'Dr Percy told me that he had heard that this pamphlet was a mere fiction written by Mr Bickerstaffe the Dramatic Poet.' I do not believe it. Dr Percy we may presume to be the vicar of Easton Maudit, Northamptonshire, and rector of Wilby in the same county, whose *Reliques of Ancient English Poetry* had become famous in 1765 and have justly remained so. Isaac Bickerstaffe, one of the first of our Irish dramatists, was a successful playwright in London between 1760 and 1771, when he fled on account of charges of sodomy, then a capital offence, for which he had earlier been deprived of a commission in the Marines. But Bickerstaffe had not been born in 1734, and Percy was only a boy of five.

If Ambrose Gwinnett had lived until 1770, he would have been eighty-one. Well, it is possible. We may have to imagine a roadsweeper of that age talking to a young Irish playwright, who was certainly not well acquainted with Deal. Men of literary note had before then compiled the autobiographies of disreputable persons from their conversation. Six years before Ambrose Gwinnett returned to Deal, Daniel Defoe had done it for Jack Sheppard.

For the purposes of our last act, we could imagine Isaac Bickerstaffe in a coffee-house near Charing Cross, at a table by a window, telling a friend about the old roadsweeper whose curious tale he had listened to up to the point at which he had been ready to leave Cuba, when he had been press-ganged by men belonging to Brian Walsh, a countryman of Bickerstaffe's, a notorious pirate. Bickerstaffe wonders whether he ought not to venture into the slums of Seven Dials in search of the old man, who was not without education.

Then we might have a last scene, with Ambrose Gwinnett dying on straw (one-legged). His last narration would be delirious.

The Stepson's Story

FRANCIS KING

WHATEVER I may have imagined at the time and have sometimes imagined since, surely Pop couldn't really have aimed at me? (I call him Pop because that's what he's always wanted me to call him and because that's what Laura, my half-sister, has always called him. He's my American stepfather, an army major who deals with catering, and he's been married for so long to my mother that I don't really remember anyone else, even though my mother often says, 'Of *course* you remember Daddy,' as though she were somehow trying to force me to do so.) I mean, why should Pop have aimed at me instead of at the man? It doesn't make any sense. He admitted in court that he was so angry and excited and confused that he had no real idea of what he was doing – 'Everything just went red' was how he described it. And, in any case, he had never had any practice in firing a gun for years – not since he first joined the Army. No, he couldn't have aimed at me. I must have imagined it; that first shot must just have gone astray.

It all happened in Holland Park more than a year ago, but I still often think about it, here in San Diego, just as I still often think about St Paul's and my English friends and our London flat. I used to love that park; it seemed to be so much larger than it really was, parts of it almost like a wood in the country. I never in the least minded taking the dog for a walk in it, even when it was raining and no one else wanted to take him. But now nothing would persuade me to go into it ever again. Sometimes I even still have nightmares about it – about that low wall and the tree with the fork in it and the rain dripping off the leaves of the tree and then those two shots. I never talk about the nightmares to Pop, because I know he wouldn't like it, and when I mention them to Mother she looks somehow worried and sad at one and the same time, and then she tells me that it's all in the past now, I must put it out of my mind and forget all about it. But it's not easy to do that. I wonder if I'll ever be able to do that.

In spite of the man I think that we were happier that summer than we'd ever been before – and, I sometimes think, than we'll ever be again. I don't like to say that, because most of the time Pop wasn't with us and it seems strange to have been so happy when, except for two or three days here and there, it was just the three of us together. Although we never admitted it to each other, and although I don't care to admit it even now, I think that we all rather dreaded Pop's returns to us from Scotland. We were so cosy together, the three of us, so cosy and comfortable. We had meals when we wanted them and we often didn't eat at home but at the new Macdonald's or at the cafeteria of the Commonwealth Institute. We didn't bother about keeping the flat too tidy, and Laura and I went to bed, not at nine as we did when Pop was around, but at any hour we felt like it. Mother would return from the telephone and say something like 'Pop will be with us on Friday; now, isn't that marvellous?' or 'Children, it's good news! We'll be having Pop home tomorrow,' but I felt – I don't know why – that she was never really as pleased and excited as she wanted us to think she was. Then we'd also pretend to be more pleased and excited than we really were. Laura would overdo it even more than I did, and I would then understand what Aunt Amy, mother's older sister, meant when she described her, more than once, as 'quite the little actress'. 'Oh, Mother!' she'd squeal in the same piercing voice that she now uses when she's talking to one of her boy-friends on the telephone. 'Oh, that's terrific! Oh, I can't believe it! Pop home again!'

Laura was very proud, even while we were still living in England, of being an American and speaking with an American accent just like Pop's. I was equally proud of being English and speaking with an English accent just like Mother's. Pop often makes fun of what he calls my 'British' or 'limey' way of talking. If, for example, at table I say, 'Could you please pass the salt?' he answers, 'Certainly, old chap! I'll be only too delighted to *pahss* anything you wish to you.' Sometimes, instead of 'old chap' he calls me 'Sir Laurence', meaning Laurence Olivier. I notice that he never makes fun of Mother's accent, even though it's exactly the same as mine. Once or twice I've said to Mother that I'm sick of Pop going on and on about the way I speak – after all, I *am* English, aren't I? But each time she's answered that I must learn not to be so sensitive, Pop likes his little joke, he just teases me out of friendliness and affection.

When Pop arrived from Scotland, he always seemed to be tired and vaguely worried. His catarrh was bad, he would complain; or he had his old back-trouble; or he wished that he could get rid of this goddamn headache. Mother would ask him why on earth he didn't take a sleeper instead of driving through the night; and then he would either say that the journey was cheaper by car and *she* ought to know how badly we needed to cut down on expenses or else that, driving alone like that for hour after hour, he found he could unwind. But he never seemed to be unwound by the time that he reached us. Just the opposite. Over breakfast he would either sit silent, staring ahead of him as he chewed and swallowed, chewed and swallowed, and gulped down coffee so hot that it made his nose go red, or else he would tell Mother about his boss, the Colonel – 'that goddamn bastard' he would often call him – and about his rows with him and about what he was going to say to him next time he handed him the same sort of shit. I had the feeling that, face to face with his boss, he always accepted the shit and said nothing at all.

Pop would go to bed after breakfast and Laura and I, if we were not at school, and if we did not want to go out, would then have to be very, very quiet. We couldn't play the hi-fi or talk except in whispers, we had to be careful not to bang the doors and we were not supposed to pull the chain or run the taps. If we forgot any of these things, we'd hear Pop groaning from the bedroom at the end of the passage, 'Oh, for Christ's sake!' and then Mother would hurry in to us and whisper that we must be more considerate, Pop was very, *very* tired.

By the time that lunch was over, he had usually recovered and I began to think that he was really a very nice stepfather to have, if one couldn't have a real father. Sometimes, it's true, he'd criticise Mother for the state of the kitchen or say that he could have eaten a better meal in the mess any day; or he'd go into my room or Linda's room and shout out, 'Do you have to live in this kind of pig-sty? Here, get this place straight! Pronto!' He'd stand over us after that, hands on hips, watching us through narrowed eyes as we tidied things up. Then, all at once he'd become jolly and friendly. 'That's my girl!' he'd say or 'That's my boy!' and he'd hug Laura or put an arm around my shoulders and then he'd suggest that maybe we'd like to go with him to this or that museum or this or that movie. We preferred the movies to the museums but we never told him that. He loves old things even though, as he often tells us, he's never been able to afford to collect them because of all his 'family obligations'. In the Victoria and Albert Museum or the British Museum he would sometimes stand for minutes on end before a show-case, watching some piece of jewellery from one of those Egyptian tombs or some piece of gold or silver from one of those Greek burial-mounds as though he expected it to move. Sometimes he would take us rowing on the Serpentine or to the Zoo or to the Planetarium or some place like that. It was fun to be with him then. I don't want to suggest that he was always silent or bad-tempered. He could be great fun, laughing and joking and mimicking people so well that it was almost uncanny to hear him.

Laura and I were much closer that summer than we had ever been before, even though we went to different schools and even though, at fifteen, I thought of myself as almost grown-up and I thought of her, four years younger, as still a child. But I sometimes got the idea that Pop didn't like us to be *too* friendly. When he wasn't there, we'd got into the habit of my going into her bedroom at night, after we'd undressed, and lying on her bed and chatting to her. When Pop learned about that, he said at once that it had to stop. I was surprised that something so unimportant should have made him so angry not only with me but also with Mother. He went quite pale and the sweat broke out on his forehead, as it always does when he loses his temper, while he told us, all three of us, not once but two or three times, that he wasn't going to have it. 'Haven't you any sense of responsibility? Are you out of your mind?' he shouted at Mother. 'How can I feel at ease up there in Scotland, when I just don't know what you're allowing to go on down here?' Mother kept calm, as she almost always does, and did not even pause in her knitting. Later, when she came to say goodnight to me, I whispered, 'He oughtn't to talk to you like that. I hate it when he does it.' She shrugged, as she stooped to put out the lamp beside my bed. Then out of the darkness I heard her: 'He's been very good to us. You mustn't forget that. Given us a lovely home. Made it possible for you to go to St Paul's instead of to a comprehensive. He flies off the handle but he doesn't really mean it. He has so much on his mind.'

Another time he found a magazine among the papers on my desk. He was looking for a rubber and then all at once, as I was watching 'Panorama' on the telly, I heard him shouting to me to go to him at once – pronto! 'Where did you get this filth?' he demanded, his face pale and those beads of sweat on his forehead. I told him that a boy at school had lent me the magazine – which was the truth. 'I won't have this kind of thing in the house! I don't care a damn what you read at school or in the park or anywhere else. But I won't have it here. Do you understand?' He began to try to tear it up, his previously pale face now turning red as he tugged at the pages. One or two pieces fell to the floor and then, stooping to pick them up, he said in a breathless voice, 'I'll have to burn it.' But before doing that he went on again: 'I will not have this kind of filth in this house. Laura might come in here and see it. She might pick it up and not know what it was. I can't have her mind exposed to that kind of – that kind of—' I waited for the word 'filth' and the word 'filth' came sure enough. Later I wondered why I had been so foolish as to leave that magazine out on my desk, when usually I hid such things under the bed or beneath a pile of clothes in my chest of drawers. It was almost as though I had *wanted* him to come on it.

Of course, since she's his very own daughter and I'm only some other man's son, Pop has always loved Laura more than me. That's only natural; it would be odd if he didn't. But he would get equally angry with both of us in those London days and he was usually far stricter with Laura than with me – which is saying a lot! All the same, I always knew that Laura was the favourite. When she was doing her homework at one end of the table in the sitting-room and I was doing mine at the other end, he would lean over her, his body against hers and a hand on her shoulder, as he looked over what she had done or told her what to do. Sometimes he would lift up a handful of the blonde hair that fell across her face – not so much, it always seemed, so that she could see her work better but so that he could see her better. When we all watched the telly – he liked the programmes about exploration and travels to foreign countries and new scientific discoveries, while Laura and I would have preferred 'Kojak' or 'Columbo' or something like that – he would call across to Laura, 'Isn't my little girl going to come to sit on Pop's knee?' and Laura would then sometimes go over and do what he said and sometimes answer in a surprisingly cross and impatient voice that it was far too hot to sit so close to another person or that she could see better where she was. He would bring us all presents from Scotland but, while to Mother or me he would say something like 'I've brought this for you' or 'You may find this useful', to Laura he would say something like 'Would my beautiful daughter like to see the lovely surprise that I've got for her?' Once he brought her a little Victorian locket shaped like a heart with a small ruby in the middle of it – it must have cost him a lot – and he himself put it around her neck, lifting up the fair hair to fasten the clasp at the back, and then he put his hands on her shoulders, looked at her and bent down and kissed her on the forehead. Of course, no father would kiss his son like that; but I couldn't help wishing that once, just once, he had looked at me with that kind of affection and tenderness.

Laura first saw the man when we were taking the spaniel, Benny, for a walk in Holland Park. We had decided to separate from each other for a little, because I wanted to watch the tennis and she wanted to go down to the playground to see if any of her school-friends were there. But then, within three or four minutes, there she was, back again. She didn't say anything, she just came and stood beside me, but as she stooped to pat the dog, I noticed that her eyes seemed to be opened more widely than usual and that her face was like Pop's when he was angry, all white and sweaty.

'Didn't you go to the playground?'

She swallowed in an odd way, as though on something bitter, and then shook her head.

'Why not?'

Still she did not speak but just shrugged her shoulders. Her lower lip was trembling now.

Soon after that we left the tennis and began to walk home. It was then that she said, 'I saw something. Something very peculiar happened to me just now.'

I asked her what, but she just shook her head.

'Go on, tell me! Don't be such an ass!'

Again she shook her head. But at last I got it out of her. 'There was this – this man. In a long grey raincoat. And a strange cap. And he looked at me in such a funny way and then he...he....' She broke off.

'Yes?' I said.

Suddenly she began to laugh and then the laughter turned to crying.

'Well?' I said. 'What was it? What did he do? What's the matter with you?' That strange laughter-crying had begun to frighten me a little.

'He – he....His – his *thing* was out!'

'What?'

'His – his *thing*!'

'Is *that* all?' I began to laugh and then the crying part of what she was doing stopped all of a sudden and she was laughing, too.

'It looked so odd,' she said. 'Weird. A kind of purple colour. And so big. It – it kind of frightened me.'

'Dirty old man!' I said, still laughing at the picture. 'You don't want to let a dirty old man like that upset you.' And 'Dirty old man!' she repeated, also still laughing.

I thought no more about it. But the next day Laura told a friend at school, a girl I never really liked, and the girl told her mother. The result was that Mrs Bacon (as she was called) telephoned to Mother and then came round. It was Laura who happened to answer the bell and, having told Mother who it was, she then rushed in to me. At the time neither of us knew about Mrs Bacon's telephone call. 'Oh Lord! Oh gosh! Oh heavens!' She put her hands up to her cheeks and swayed from side to side, as she still does when she's embarrassed or upset.

'What is it?'

'It's Mrs Bacon.'

'And who's she?'

'Angela's mother.'

'What's she come about?' I was wishing that Laura would leave me alone to get on with a watch I was trying to repair.

Laura did not reply. Instead she threw herself face downwards on my bed, still saying 'Oh Lord! Oh gosh! Oh heavens!' and things like that and wriggling about like a fish that's just been hooked. I got up and went into the sitting-room to have a peep at this Mrs Bacon.

The two of them stopped talking as I appeared. Mrs Bacon – who, I later learned, was some kind of social worker – had fat arms and legs and a large bosom that jutted out, quite close to her chin, like a shelf. Her face, under a bright-red hat shaped like a coal-scuttle, looked hot and no less red. 'What do you want, dear?' Mother asked and, before I had time to answer, went on: 'This is my son.'

'Oh, yes, I've heard about him,' Mrs Bacon said in a voice that suggested that all she had heard might not be good.

'I was looking for my trigonometry book,' I said after I had shaken her hand. The hand seemed strangely cold in contrast to the hotness of her face.

'It doesn't seem to be here,' Mother said, looking vaguely around her. 'Now, could you leave us alone for a little, there's a dear? We have something private to discuss.'

I left them and went back to my room, where I found Laura now sitting up on my bed, her back against the wall. She began to gnaw at a thumb-nail – something that always made Pop angry. 'What were they saying?' she asked. I told her I didn't know but that Mother had asked me to leave the room and had said that it was something private. 'Oh lordy!' She now began to gnaw at the nail on her forefinger.

'What's this all about?'

She shook her head.

'Tell me.'

Finally I got it out of her. 'That man,' she said.

'What man?'

'That man in Holland Park.'

'Oh, that! But what has Mrs Bacon ...?'

'I told Angela about it.'

After Mrs Bacon had gone, we expected Mother to say something. But she went into the kitchen, where we heard her moving about as she fried some sausages and mixed some Smash for our supper. 'Children!' she eventually called. As we ate, she still said nothing, but she was unusually silent, putting now one elbow and now the other and sometimes both on the table, in the way that she was so often telling us not to sit at meal-times. She looked thoughtful more than troubled.

A few days later Pop came home. He was even more tired and in an even worse temper than usual because he had had a puncture on the way. We tiptoed round the flat and then, even though the rain was coming down in buckets, we wandered out with Benny. He had to be dragged along the High Street and kept trying to take shelter under the awnings of shops. When we returned home, just before lunch-time, we heard Pop shouting at Mother in the bedroom as we opened the door. 'Good God, woman, didn't you go to the police?'

We remained without moving in the small, square, high-ceilinged hall that was so dark, with its frosted window on to the well of the block, that it was as though we were standing in a cellar. We didn't hear Mother's answer.

Pop went on: 'And didn't you tell her never to go into that goddamn park again?'

This time we heard: 'No. After all, it's not likely to happen again.'

'It could easily happen again. What do you mean? That kind of pervert tends to hang around the same place, just like a dog going back to the same lamp-post.'

Mother said something inaudible and then, her voice louder now: 'One doesn't want to make too much of it.'

'Make too much of it! One can't make too much of it!' Laura had begun to gnaw at a thumb-nail. I wanted to stop her. Pop would notice, as he always did, and that would make him even crosser. 'That kind of pervert is a menace to any child that goes into the goddamn park.'

'She'll forget about it. If it had made any real impression on her, I'd have known. By talking about it – by making a fuss about it....'

'For Chrissake!' Pop bellowed that.

I shut the front door noisily behind us, at which Mother said, 'Sh! There they are – back from their walk!'

'Well, tell them to come and see me. Now. Here. Pronto!'

Pop still lay under the bedclothes, his chin blue because he hadn't shaved yet, his eyes bleary and one side of his face creased, as though with a scar, where he had been lying on it. 'Come here, Laura baby,' he said, patting the eiderdown beside him. 'Pop wants a word with his little girl.' I knew that Laura was frightened and that she did not want to go and sit that close to Pop. But she walked over, slightly zigzag and knock-kneed in the way that always meant that she was shy or nervous, and sat upright beside him, her legs dangling over the side of the bed. He pulled her towards him, so that she now rested against his shoulder. 'Laura honey,' he said. 'Mother tells me something nasty happened to you in the park.' Laura did not answer. 'Laura?'

Mother, who was standing by the door, next to me, cut in: 'Oh, do leave it!' She was on the verge of crying, I could tell.

'Laura, are you listening to me? Is my little girl really and truly listening? Now, if anything like that happens again, ever, *ever*, I want you to look and see if you can find one of those keepers or a policeman. And, if you can't, well, honey, just tell one of the other people in the park – one of the grown-ups, I mean – and he or she will know exactly what to do. And if there's no one handy in the park, then just you come home, straight home as quick as you can run, and tell Mother all about it. Got it? Laura? Now, don't bite your nails, honey! You know how Pop hates you to spoil your lovely little hands. Laura!' He gave her a sharp little shake with the arm that was still around her and, like a doll's, her head flopped forward and then back again.

'Now, son.' I had been dreading this all the time that I had been standing by the door. He put up a hand and beckoned and, step by step, I approached him, as though with that beckoning finger he was pulling on a string attached to me.

'Yes, Pop.' I had to clear my throat before I spoke.

'Did you see this guy?'

'No, Pop.'

'How come?'

'What do you mean?'

'Well – just that. How come? Weren't you and Laura there together?'

'Yes, Pop.... But – well – we'd separated.'

'You mean you left your little sister while you wandered off some place?'

'No, Pop. I mean ... I wanted to watch the tennis and she wanted to go to the playground to see if – if any of her friends were there.'

'I see. I get the picture.' He seemed about to say something else but instead stared at me so intensely, almost as though he were accusing me of something, that I felt the sweat breaking out all over my body. 'Now, look, son. So that you can go on going to that fine expensive school of yours and so that little Laura can go on going to hers, I've had to make big, big sacrifices. I've had to leave you all down here in London and I've had to go and live in unmarried quarters up there in Scotland without Mother to look after me. Now, haven't I? Well, when I'm away, I've got to be able to feel that I can rely on you to take my place. I mean, it's worrying enough as it is, me being so far away and not knowing from one moment to the next how you all are making out down here. I've got to be able to rely on you to look after your baby sister.' Again he stared at me and again I felt hot and sticky all over my body. Mother's arm was suddenly around my shoulders, but somehow I didn't want it there because – I don't know why – I felt that that might make things even worse for me with Pop. And I think that I was right, because he at once asked, not in the soft, sorrowful kind of voice that he had been using so far, but sharply, 'Didn't Laura tell you what had happened to her?'

'Yes, Pop.' Again I had to clear my throat before I could answer.

'And didn't you go and look for this man?'

'No, Pop.'

'You didn't feel you should go and look for him and

ask him what the hell it was that he was doing to your little sister?'

'I suppose I thought ... I thought it was too late by then to find him.'

'You *supposed*! Fine!...Look, son, you're almost a man now. A man would have gone and knocked a degenerate like that down.'

Mother was trying to draw me closer to her, but I resisted.

'You didn't even think of looking for one of those park-attendants?' Silence. 'Or a policeman?' Silence. 'Hell, what kind of brother are you?'

Mother began, 'He probably never realised—' but Pop cut her short:

'You never even told your mother, your own mother!'

He threw his legs out of the bed, his arm still about Laura's waist. I saw that he was wearing nothing but his vest and underpants. Somehow, though I had often seen him like that before, I was now realising for the first time how thin and hairy his legs were. 'Well, I guess it's about time for chow.' Suddenly he had become good-humoured and smiling. 'What have you got for us, Mother?'

Mother mumbled, 'Steak-and-kidney pie.'

'Steak-and-kidney pie as only Mother can make it!' Mother always bought frozen steak-and-kidney pie, but neither she nor Laura nor I ever let on. 'Now, Laura honey, Pop must get dressed.' Laura clambered off the bed, her lower lip trembling and her eyelashes blinking as though, as on that day when she saw the man, she did not know whether to laugh or cry. He got to his feet. 'Now, Laura, if anything like this happens again, you know what Pop wants you to do?'

'Yes, Pop.'

'And, son, you've got it straight now, haven't you?'

'Yes, Pop.'

'We've got to get the police to act on this pronto, if it

ever happens again. Otherwise some other little girl is going to be exposed to the same kind of filth. Or worse. In fact, after lunch I'm going to put on my uniform and I'm going along to see the police to tell them. They ought to be warned.... OK. Now, run along, all of you. And make sure, Mother, that I have a big, big serving of that steak-and-kidney pie of yours. Don't let the kids eat all of it before I get to it!'

Laura usually walked home from school across Holland Park. If she didn't, it meant going all the way down Holland Walk, along Kensington High Street and then up Melbury Road. Angela – whose home, a big house, not a flat, was in the street next to ours – often walked with her. But she and Laura were always having silly little tiffs and then Laura would walk with someone else for a day or two. Because she was so pretty and so good at netball, and perhaps also because she spoke with that American accent, there was always a lot of competition for this honour.

About ten days after Pop had spoken to us about the man, I had just got back from St Paul's and was having a cup of tea with Mother in the kitchen, when Laura rushed in. (Each of us had a key to the front door, since Mother so often went out to visit the aunts.) At first, from her excited face, I thought that she must have some good news from school – there was to be an unexpected holiday, she had come top of her form, she had been invited to a party or away for the weekend. But instead she cried out, 'It's happened again! It's happened again! He did it again!'

Mother got to her feet, her cup still in her hand. She looked horribly upset, but I had the feeling – I don't know why – that she was even more upset by Laura's excitement than by its cause. 'Now, take off your hat and put your satchel down. Then come and sit here and tell me.'

'But, Mother, he did it again! And Pop said—'

'Come and sit down, dear,' Mother repeated in a soft but firm voice. She pulled out a chair.

Laura sat on it, right on the edge. Her eyes were as bright as that time when she had had a high fever with measles.

'Were you alone?' Mother asked.

'Yes. Angela was going to walk with me but then Miss Barlow called her back about her music-lesson and so I thought I wouldn't wait for her. And then—'

'Weren't there any other girls you could have walked with?'

'They'd all set off by then. I thought I might catch someone up.' She gnawed at a thumb-nail. I could hear the click-click-click of her teeth on it. 'Oh, Mother, it was *horrible*!'

'Now, tell me – quietly and calmly – exactly what happened, dear.'

'Well, I was walking along, just beyond the Youth Hostel. I was walking quite fast. And then – then – well, there he was!'

'Where, dear?'

'In the bushes. And he opened his raincoat, this long grey raincoat, and then....' Suddenly she began to sob, her arms crossed on the kitchen table and her cheek resting on them.

Mother sighed, looked at me and then got up. Her face was sad and somehow distant, as though she were thinking not of what had just happened but of something long ago. 'Darling. Darling. Now, come along.' She was stooping over Laura. 'It's not all that bad or all that important.' Laura continued to sob loudly. 'Are you sure it was the same man?'

Laura jerked up. 'Don't you believe me?' she wailed.

'Of course I believe you, darling, but are you sure...?'

'Of course I'm sure! He – he was wearing this same grey raincoat; it's a long raincoat, grey, oh, almost to his ankles – no, not almost to his ankles but, oh, far below his knees. And glasses – the sun was on them so I couldn't see his eyes, though I knew that he was staring at me. And this funny cap, a cap with a peak, like – like a schoolboy's almost – like that one that Angela's brother wears. Of *course* it was the same man! Oh, Mother, it was *horrible*! Beastly! I wish Pop was here!'

The mention of Pop seemed to make Mother stiffen and straighten in her chair, as though she had remembered something suddenly. 'Give her some tea or orange juice,' she said to me. 'Look after her. I'm just going to the telephone.'

'Where are you going to telephone?' Laura asked. But Mother left the room without giving any answer.

'Do you want some tea?' I asked. I felt embarrassed and not at all sure how to cope with Laura by herself. It was as though she had suddenly become a stranger.

She shook her head and then put out a hand and began to stir the sugar, slowly round and round, in the bowl. 'You believe me, don't you?'

I nodded. 'Why not? Why should you lie about it or make it up?' I could hear Mother talking on the telephone in the next room but I couldn't hear what she was saying.

'You probably think this is all a lot of fuss about nothing.'

It was, in fact, what I did think, but I shook my head.

'It's difficult for a boy to understand.'

Mother came back. 'The police'll be here as soon as possible.'

'The police!' Laura was terrified. 'Oh, Mother!'

'Pop said that I must ring them. Don't you remember? They sounded very nice and understanding.'

'Oh, but I wish....'

'I had to do what Pop told us to do.'

In no time at all there was a ring at the bell and there were these two policemen, one old and slightly shrivelled and grey-looking, with a West Country accent, and the other square-shouldered and young, with long reddish hair that reached over his collar and a straggling reddish moustache that all but covered his small irregular teeth. I must say they were very polite and sympathetic, talking in the kind of quiet voices that people use when you are ill and addressing Mother as 'mam' and Laura as 'miss'. After they had been told how everything had happened, the older one asked Laura and Mother to go with them in the car to see if they could spot the man in the park.

'Oh, but he's sure to have gone by now,' Mother said as though she were not at all eager to go with them.

'You never know, mam,' the older policeman said. 'You just can't say in these cases. Sometimes they hang about waiting for another victim. You can't expect them to behave as an ordinary person would.'

'It's worth a try,' said the other one.

'There's nothing to be afraid of, miss. We'll be there to protect you. All we want is for you to point him out if you spot him.'

The four of them eventually left and I tried to settle to my homework. But I felt restless and somehow uneasy, and so eventually I took one of the cigarettes from the box in the sitting-room and smoked that while looking out of the window for their return. I opened the window wide and hoped that Mother wouldn't smell anything.

After about half an hour the car drew up at the kerb and Mother and Laura got out. Mother said something I couldn't hear to the men inside the car, and then I heard the young one's voice as he leaned out of the window, booming at her so that any neighbour who was around could have heard: 'Well, don't hesitate to call us if it ever happens again. That's what we're here for.' I knew then that they hadn't been able to find the man and I threw what was left of the cigarette out of the window and hurried back to my homework.

'Well?' I asked, looking up as they came in.

'No sign of him,' Mother sighed.

'I knew he wouldn't be there any longer,' Laura said. 'It was just a waste of time.'

'Well, there was nothing else they could do. They did their best. They were really very helpful and nice.'

'I *hated* the younger one!'

'Don't be silly! Why should you hate him?'

'I think he thought I'd imagined it all.'

'I don't think he thought anything of the kind.' Mother looked tired and pale. She went and flopped down in one of the two armchairs, the one that Pop usually used, and stared into the empty grate with its fan of greying paper. 'I've been thinking,' she said. 'Perhaps it would be better not to tell Pop all about this. It'll only upset him. You know how tired he always is on his visits.' She did not look at either of us, and neither of us said anything. 'Children?'

'As you like, Mother,' I replied.

Laura said nothing.

I think that I knew even then that Laura would not do as Mother asked. I'm not sure exactly how she came to tell Pop – whether he asked her or whether she volunteered – but she had been in his room, after he had woken from his sleep but was still lying in bed, and then, all at once, there he was, his hair standing on end and his face all red and crumpled, shouting in nothing but his vest and underpants and a pair of socks that were hanging round his ankles. 'Mother! Mother! Come here, will you!'

Mother came out of the kitchen, where she had been at work on the lunch, and I put my head round the door to see what the row was all about. Pop squinted at me in a puzzled, vaguely hostile way. 'Did I call for you, son?' he demanded.

'No, Pop.'

'Well, then, beat it!'

I disappeared behind the door and gave it a little push, so as not to shut it completely.

I heard: 'Laura's just been telling me that that goddamn bastard has been up to his tricks again.'

I could hear no answer from Mother; perhaps she merely nodded.

'Well, for Christ's sake, why didn't you tell me? Don't I have a right to know? I've telephoned here, oh, at least half a dozen times and you've said not a word.'

'I didn't want to upset you – worry you. You've so much else on your mind.'

'I haven't so much on my mind that I don't need to worry about my little girl having another experience of that kind. Are you crazy?'

'I called the police at once. Just as you told me.'

'And a hell of a lot of good they seem to have been!'

'They did their best. They came here in a car and then they—'

'Yeah, yeah! I've heard it all from Laura. It turns me up, the whole thing turns me up. Christ, what's happening to this country?'

He went on for a long, long time like that, until Mother said, quietly but firmly, that she must get back to the kitchen or else the lunch would get spoiled.

Pop ate a huge lunch and, as so often after he has made one of his scenes, he was in the best of moods. He even poured me out some beer when he poured out some for himself and he kept us all laughing with some long story about 'two long-haired hippies' who had thumbed a hitch-hike from him. Lunch over, he belched loudly, making Laura and me laugh even more than at the end of the story, and then he smacked a knee with either palm and said, 'Well, kids, how about it? I want to see this Bicentennial Exhibition at Greenwich. Are you both game?'

Neither of us was too keen to see the Exhibition, but Laura screeched, 'Oh, Pop! How terrific!' and I said, 'Fine!'

It was a sunny day, but a cold wind was blowing; and Pop, who always felt the cold more than any of us – he was always saying 'this weather in Britain gets into my bones' – told us that we should go downstairs into the saloon of the boat to Greenwich. 'Oh, but Pop, we won't be able to see anything from there!' Laura protested, but he said that he didn't want his little girl running around with a runny nose or in bed with a chill and she was to be a good girl and do what he told her. 'Now, would you believe that! Christ!' he exclaimed, looking around the saloon, which was empty but for a single elderly couple who were sitting up very stiff and straight with quite a distance between them. 'Well!' He meant that the bar had an iron grille across it and there was not a chance of a drink. He got a hip-flask out of his trousers and took a swig from that. Bourbon. That was always his drink in England as it is now in the States. He wiped his mouth on the back of his hand, apparently unaware that the elderly couple had been staring at him in disapproval, and then sat down on the cracked leather seat that ran along the wall on the other side. 'Well, is my best girl going to sit beside me?' Laura sat down next to him; but she was soon up again, kneeling on the seat in order to look out of the port-hole. I remained standing. It was stuffy down there and everything smelled of diesel-oil and stale cigarette-smoke. I began to feel slightly sick.

When we had been travelling for about five minutes, Laura said, 'Pop, mayn't I just go up on deck for the teeniest weeniest while? I can't see *at all* from here.' She had been sitting down and then jumping up again and rushing from port-hole to port-hole.

'OK, honey. But make it short and sweet. And this brother of yours had better tag along to keep an eye on you. Don't lean over the rail and don't talk to any of those foreign students I saw up there, even if they talk to you.'

'Thanks, Pop. 'Bye!'

She ran up the companionway, and I followed after her. Pop shouted something about not taking her cardigan off, but either she did not hear him or she pretended not to hear.

It was such fun up on deck, trying to recognise one landmark after another – the Houses of Parliament, the dome of St Paul's, the Monument, Wapping Old Stairs – and watching the little motorboats and the barges and the sailing dinghies, that we both forgot all about Pop. We even forgot what he had told us about not talking to the students. One of them, a skinny boy of about my age, in shorts and a tee-shirt – his knobbly knees and elbows and knuckles were blue with cold – pointed to the Hayward Gallery and said, in a French accent, 'Excuse me – prison?' and then we corrected him and we all began laughing and so we got into conversation with the whole lot of them.

Suddenly Pop was there, the wind blowing his trousers tight against his legs and his hair over to one side so that one could see the bald patch that he usually kept hidden. 'Laura!' he bawled. At that moment he seemed to be angrier with her than with me. 'Now, what did I tell you? This is a nice way to behave when I take you on a treat!' He looked at her. '*And* you've undone that cardigan.'

'Oh, Pop, I'm sorry, but it was so lovely up here and really not at all cold, not at all cold, Pop.'

'Well, what do you think it was like for me down below – all on my own while you two were fooling around up here together? You'd forgotten all about your Pop – now, hadn't you? He might have been miles and miles away in Scotland for all you cared.'

'Oh, Pop!' She ran to him and took his hand, pressing her cheek against his windcheater, and I could see that, though he was now squinting at me in that way of his when I had made him angry, he was going to forgive us. 'OK, OK!' he said. 'But Pop has certainly got himself a very, very disobedient little sweetheart.' He ran a hand through her hair, and at that same moment the boat let out a long wail. We were about to dock.

The next time that Laura said that she had seen the man, she had been with Angela. The two girls ran back to the school – because it was nearer than their homes, they said – and told the headmistress what had happened, She at once telephoned to the police and again a police-car hurried over. The crew were different from the other time – 'much nicer', Laura said. The two men and the two girls drove round and round the park, even going up and down paths meant only for pedestrians, but the man had vanished as before.

Mrs Bacon again visited Mother, bringing Angela with her but sending her into Laura's room while the two mothers talked. From my room it was impossible to hear what they were saying to each other; but at the door, as she was leaving – I was in the hall, too – she turned to Mother. 'Well, if you don't feel inclined to come and see Miss Pratt with me, at least I can tell her that you agree with me one hundred per cent, can't I?'

'What are you going to see Miss Pratt about?' Angela asked, looking across at Laura and then, when she caught her eye, putting a hand up to cup her mouth as though she were going either to giggle or cough.

'Never mind, dear.' Mrs Bacon turned once more to Mother. 'I can say that we're completely at one over this?'

Mother looked doubtful, as she said in a flat tired voice, 'Oh, yes, I think so.'

'Good,' Mrs Bacon said firmly. 'Then, I'll see her first thing tomorrow.'

Later I learned that Mrs Bacon had asked the headmistress to tell all the girls not to go into the park, but that Miss Pratt had thought this 'altogether too drastic' since there had been only two reported incidents of that kind to date. Mrs Bacon told Mother this in the forecourt outside Barkers, where we had run into her while the two of us were doing the weekend shopping. I was carrying Mother's basket, making Mrs Bacon comment: 'How nice to have a stalwart young man to do one's carrying for one!' She was wearing another coal-scuttle hat, this time bright blue, not red, with a spray of feathers, dyed a darker blue, pinned to one side. 'That woman is quite incapable of any kind of decisive action. She just dithers.' She was talking about Miss Pratt, but it seemed to me almost as if she were talking about Mother, and Mother seemed to feel that, too, as she began to blush and look uneasy. 'It was the same when those boys from the comprehensive used to shout things over the wall. Hopeless. Well, at all events, I've told my Angela that from now on she's not to set foot in the park. That's flat.'

'It's an awful long way round to the school for them,' Mother said. 'And worse back after a tiring day.'

'Well, better an extra quarter of an hour than a repetition,' Mrs Bacon said firmly, shifting her basket from one hand to the other. She leaned forward to Mother and lowered her voice as though she thought that that was enough to prevent my hearing: 'I do think that exhibitionism is such an extraordinary thing. I always have. It's the only sexual – er – peculiarity that is turned entirely against its object. Isn't it? There's no desire to attract, the purpose is not to achieve any kind of – er – communication. Just the opposite. What it does is disgust and repel.'

Mother nodded, gave me a nervous glance and nodded again.

As we left Mrs Bacon, Mother sighed: 'Oh dear.' She made no other comment.

*

When Pop came home the following weekend and learned that the man had shown himself to Laura yet again, he became even more frantic than on the other occasions. Instead of going to bed after breakfast, he stormed at Mother for most of the morning. Why hadn't she spoken to the police herself? Why hadn't she gone with Mrs Bacon to see Miss Pratt? Why hadn't she forbidden Laura to go into the park again? He kept pouring out beer for himself – he had taken off his jacket and shirt and in spite of that he was sweating freely – and, as he gulped it down, glass after glass, he kept thinking of something fresh to say. I felt sorry for him – almost as sorry for him as for Mother. He kept repeating how terrible it was for him to be so far away, up there in that goddamn place way out in the sticks, not knowing what was happening to his loved ones, not able to protect them, not able to guide them. Eventually Mother began to cry and then, between sobs, she told me to go to my room and Laura to go to hers. Or else, she said, we could have a walk before lunch. 'But not in that park, for Christ's sake, not in that park!' Pop took his head out of his hands to shout. 'Because that boy is certainly not going to be able to cope with the situation if that maniac appears.' Laura had all this time been playing patience in a corner on the floor. She had not seemed to be interested at all in what was going on, and when we were out in the street and I said, 'What a lot of fuss! It's given me quite a headache,' she only said, ignoring my remark, 'There's no reason why we shouldn't go to Kensington Gardens. We can watch all those silly old men flying kites.'

That night, after we had been sent to bed at nine, I could hear Pop going on and on at Mother in the next room even though I could seldom hear what she was saying. 'I know about these things.... Well, for Pete's sake, I did a course in psychiatry in college – which is more than you ever did.... A shock like that can turn off a young girl for life....Well, of course it can!...Of *course*!...Everyone knows that....It can make her goddamn frigid for life....Half these frigid women have had some kind of shock like that way back in their childhoods. It's been proved....And I want my little Laura to grow up into a thoroughly normal healthy woman....Is that too much for a father to want for his daughter?...Well, is it? Is it?'

I pulled the bedclothes over my head and decided to go to sleep.

Laura now had to walk the long way to and from school, and that meant that she had to set off earlier and came back later. I guessed that on some days, especially when it was raining or when she didn't want to miss some programme on the telly, she disobeyed Pop's orders and cut across the park. I suspect that Angela also sometimes disobeyed Mrs Bacon. Certainly, one afternoon when I was taking the dog for a walk after I had come home from school, I saw the two girls coming out of the lower gate. They looked surprised and disconcerted and for a moment I even thought that they were going to pretend that they hadn't noticed me so near to them. 'I thought that you'd been strictly forbidden to go into the park,' I said, not seriously but to tease them.

'We just slipped in to see about that pop concert in the open-air theatre on Sunday afternoon,' Angela put in quickly. 'That was all. Only for a moment. You won't tell on us, will you?'

'Of course not.'

'There was no sign of *him*,' Laura said.

'Thank goodness,' Angela added. Then they both began to giggle.

'D'you want to come back in with me and the dog?'

'Oh, no! We'd better not,' Angela said.

'We daren't!' Laura added. 'Pop told me that, even with you, I was never to go in. And Mr and Mrs Bacon both told Angela that on no account—'

'Please yourselves!' I said. I was quite glad not to have them with me, whispering and giggling together and making remarks to each other that I usually did not understand and did not wish to understand.

It was two or three days after that that Laura came back from school accompanied by a thin, spectacled, middle-aged woman in a shabby coat with one button hanging loose on its front. 'I've brought your little girl back home,' she said when Mother answered the ring at the door. 'She seems to have had a rather nasty little experience.' Laura stood behind her, as though for protection. I wondered why she hadn't opened the door with her key. 'I expect she'll tell you all about it herself,' the woman went on.

'Oh, not again!' Mother gasped.

'Has it happened before? Oh, my word!'

Laura looked quite calm as she now came out from behind the woman, put down her satchel and began to take off her hat and blazer.

Mother nodded. 'Yes, I'm afraid so. More than once.'

'I looked to see if the dirty brute was still there – she said he was in one of those telephone kiosks just at the end of Kensington Walk – but of course he'd beat it. Just as well! If I'd got my hands on him—'

'I'm awfully grateful to you,' Mother said.

'The little girl wanted to call the police,' the woman went on, first fiddling with the dangling button and then giving it a sharp tug so that it came away in her hand. 'But, since he was no longer there, there didn't seem any point. Besides – to be absolutely truthful with you – I'm hurrying home to get my old man his tea and I'll be late as it is.'

'Oh, I *am* sorry!' Mother said. 'Oh dear!'

'Not to worry. He'll have to wait for a change. I'll hop on the 28 outside the Odeon.'

By now Laura had gone into the kitchen and had started to pour out for herself some orange juice from the jug in the fridge. Mother followed her there and I came in behind her. She watched Laura for a time as though uncertain how to begin. Then she said, 'Laura dear.'

'Yes, Mother.' Laura sipped daintily. The sunshine through the window glinted on her fair hair and on one of her cheekbones, and I thought: Yes, Pop *is* right when he's always telling her how pretty she is.

'Laura. I want you to be absolutely truthful with me.'

'Yes, Mother.' She sipped again.

'Did you really see that man or did you...?' She faltered there.

'Yes, Mother?'

'Or did you just imagine it?'

'Imagine, Mother? Why should I imagine it? *Of course* I saw him. It was broad daylight, you know that, and there he was in the kiosk and, as I passed, he opened the door and then he opened that horrible long grey raincoat – by then he was holding the door open with a foot – and – and—'

'All right, dear.'

'Don't you *believe* me, Mother?' Suddenly she banged the glass of half-finished orange juice down on the table, so hard that I thought she would break it, and no less suddenly there were tears in her eyes.

'Of course, darling!' Mother put an arm round her. 'It was a beastly experience. Now, I want you to forget all about it.'

'But I can't, I can't!' Laura wailed.

'Now, Laura.... Please.... Don't be silly....'

Laura was sobbing helplessly, and no less helplessly Mother looked across at me. But I had no idea what to do about it. I knew that Pop would get even more frantic when he heard of this latest appearance of the man, and of course I was right.

*

Pop was having ten days' leave when the man showed himself to Laura for the last time. It had been raining all afternoon, a steady downpour, and for the first time one realised that another summer was over. Mother had come into the sitting-room, where I was busy with my homework and Pop was reading a detective-novel, and had hugged herself in the way that she does when she is cold and had asked whether we didn't want the fire on. But Pop said no, she knew that we had to economise, if she was that cold why didn't she put on a sweater or cardigan? Mother replied in a soft distant voice, 'I was thinking of you. You always feel the cold more than the rest of us,' and Pop then said, 'Well, thanks, honey,' in a tone that might or might not have been sarcastic.

A little later Pop stirred in the armchair, took out a handkerchief and blew his nose loudly – he had been complaining again of his catarrh – and then looked at his watch and asked, 'What's happened to that little girl of mine?'

I did not answer, since he seemed to be putting the question to himself and not to me, and then he said, '*You* don't care, do you?'

I looked up from my work, surprised, and said, 'Don't care what?'

'*You* don't care a fuck what's happened to her!' I did not answer. 'No, of course you don't. Boy, what a brother!'

It was only a few seconds after that that there was a ring at the bell, followed at once by the sound of a key in the lock of the front door. 'What the hell—?' Pop jumped to his feet, the detective-story in one hand, and at the same moment Laura ran in. 'He did it again, he did it again!' she screamed, running up to Pop and throwing her arms around him. 'Oh, Pop! He was there!'

'Where?' Pop asked. 'Where, Laura? Where?'

Mother came in at all this commotion, looked at

them both and said, 'Laura! You haven't been in that park!'

Laura began to sob, still clutching at Pop. 'I had to go that way. It's pouring outside and I hadn't got a mac or an umbrella or anything. I'm soaked. Look at me!'

'I told you to take your mac this morning at breakfast,' Mother said.

'What the hell is the use of telling the kid that now?' Pop shouted at her. 'Here, Laura, wait a sec. We're going to find him. This time we're going to get him! These goddamn British cops are no fucking use. We'll get him together, sweetie.' He ran out of the room, into the bedroom that he and Mother shared, and Mother followed him. I heard her cry out, 'What are you doing? What d'you want that thing for? Pop!' But he just shouted at her, 'Oh, get lost!'

He was putting something into the pocket of his service raincoat as he came out. 'Come on, Laura! Come on, sweetie! Come with Pop!'

'You're not taking her with you?' Mother said.

'Certainly I'm taking her with me. How the fucking else am I to recognise the bastard?'

'But she's all wet,' Mother said.

Pop paid no attention to that. He looked at me. 'And you, too.'

'Me?'

'Yeah, you. Not that you're likely to be of much help to me, Sir Laurence. *Move!* Come on, *move*!'

I got up and went into the hall.

'Take your mac,' Mother said. 'And you, too, Laura.' I took mine down from the peg, but Laura did not seem to have heard. Mother went on: 'Look, you don't need to drag the children into all this—'

But Pop wasn't listening. 'Come on, honey!' He put an arm round Laura's shoulders and pushed her out of the front door. Then he made a gesture with his head at me. 'OK. Out. Pronto.'

He told me to get into the back of the car and Laura to get in front beside him. There was a lot of cursing under his breath as the engine died on him two or three times. 'Too much choke, too much fucking choke,' he muttered. Then, at last, we were moving. 'Now, honey, you tell Pop exactly where he was. Because Pop is going to find that bastard, come what may.'

Laura didn't seem to be in the least bit frightened now. I was amazed by her calmness as she directed him: 'This way, Pop,' or 'Turn right, Pop.' Finally she said, 'He was up there, Pop. But cars can't go there.'

'Like hell they can't!' Pop muttered between his teeth, and the car began lurching up the narrow path between dripping bushes. Because of the heavy rain, we saw no one but a man with an umbrella, with a little dog, all huddled up, trailing behind him on a lead. 'Is that him?' Pop demanded, and Laura replied, with a little giggle, 'No, Pop. He doesn't look at all like that. Like I said, he has this long grey raincoat and this funny cap.'

I don't think I really believed that the man had been in the park that afternoon with all that rain – I was sure that Laura had imagined it all or had made it up as some weird kind of joke – when suddenly there he was, about two hundred yards ahead of us, walking quickly up the path, his hands deep in the pockets of the raincoat and his shoulders hunched, just as she had described him.

'That's him, Pop!' Laura cried out excitedly. 'That's him! There in front of us!'

'Are you sure?'

'Of course I'm sure! It's the raincoat and the cap and the way he....Oh, Pop!'

As though without looking round, the man knew that we were driving up closer and closer behind him and were not on the road on the other side of the fence, he all at once left this path for another, narrower, one that wound into the woods. It was impossible to follow him any longer in the car. Pop braked sharply. 'Now, Laura,' he said, 'I want you to be a good girl and do what Pop tells you. As soon as we leave this car, I want you to lock it all round. Got that? *Lock it all round!* 'Cos I don't want anything nasty to happen to my little girl.' He looked over his shoulder at me. 'OK. Out!' I hesitated. '*Out!*'

We plunged down the path, Pop lurching from time to time so that the bushes made a swishing sound against his army raincoat. He was gaining on the man and leaving me behind him. Then the man began to run and Pop began to run, too. I trotted behind them. I didn't really want to be there when Pop caught him up.

Pop is no athlete – even then he had this small pot in front, I suppose from all that beer-drinking – but the man was really feeble. He darted from one side to another, just as I saw a mouse doing when Benny cornered it in the hall, and I could hear him cry out in his high-pitched educated voice, 'What do you want? Who are you? What is it? Please!'

Pop had grabbed him. 'This is a citizen's arrest,' he said. 'So you'd better come quietly. Or else.'

The man wriggled in his grip. 'I don't understand. What do you mean? What is this all about?' Now he was whimpering. He wore thick glasses with heavy steel frames and they were all dotted with raindrops. I wondered how much he could see of us.

'You've been molesting my little girl,' Pop said. 'That's what you've been doing. She's back there in that locked car over there and she's picked you out for me. There's no doubt about it. No doubt at all!'

In a husky voice, no longer whimpering, the man said, 'All right. All right. I'll come. But just let me go. You're hurting my arm. I don't know what. I don't know why.' He pushed the glasses up his nose with one hand and I saw that the sleeve of the raincoat was too long, covering the hand almost to the finger-tips. 'All right.' He was still out of breath and so was Pop. Both their faces looked yellow in the gloom under the dripping trees, and the cap was all sodden, so that it looked as though it had a stain in the middle of it. Pop's hair lay in wet prongs on his forehead.

'OK', Pop said to me. 'Get the other side of him. We don't want any funny stuff.' I stood on one side of the man and Pop was on the other. Suddenly Pop had become strangely calm, almost as though he were stupefied. 'I have to do this,' he said. 'You see that, don't you?' He might have been apologising.

The man's reply surprised me. In that high-pitched educated voice he said, 'And I have to do it, too. Can't help myself.' We had begun to walk. 'It's terrible. Terrible really. I've been in trouble before. Not here, in Eastbourne. And before that, oh, years ago, I was only a student, in a cinema at Oxford. I'm a married man. Three kids. I don't know why. I don't know how. A compulsion. Can't get away from it.' He was still breathless and the words came out in spurts.

Pop sounded sympathetic as he answered, 'Yeah. OK. But you can't do that kind of thing to a little girl. Not to a little girl like my Laura. How can you dirty up a young life as fine and pure as that? Christ! I mean, I see you've got your problem, but Christ—!'

Suddenly the man halted and put his hands to his stomach, hunching himself over as he did so. 'Oh God!' he said. 'Oh!' His face looked even yellower.

'What's the matter?' Pop asked, still in that strangely sympathetic tone.

'I think. I think that. I think that I'm. Going to be sick.' His face was screwed up now and the words again came out in spurts.

'Well, don't throw up on us!' Pop shouted, and suddenly all the sympathy had disappeared and he sounded angry and vindictive once again. 'Go and throw up over there!'

The man started gagging. Then he took a few steps away from us and started gagging again. Then he took a few more steps and some saliva glistened as it shot from his mouth and dribbled down his chin. Long before Pop I knew what he was planning and I was ready for him. All at once he raced for the tree by the wall.

I was amazed that that middle-aged, narrow-shouldered, breathless man should suddenly show so much speed and agility. He jumped into the fork of the tree and then a hand went out, half-concealed by the sleeve of the long grey raincoat, and reached for the top of the wall. 'Get him!' Pop shouted. 'Go on! Get him!' But I had already got him by one leg and was pulling at him. Then I heard Pop shout, 'Don't move! Don't move! If you move, you've had it!' I turned my head, still holding the man's leg with one hand and a tail of his raincoat with the other. Then I saw what Pop was holding in his hand. 'It's all right!' I shouted. 'Pop!' Pop was squinting at me (however I try to remember it differently, he is always squinting at me and not at the man) in the way that he does even now when he's angry with me. 'Pop!' I shouted again. He was still squinting at me. Then the gun exploded. I let go of the man and began to run away. I remember thinking as I ran: Am I alive? Am I still alive? Has he wounded me? Then I heard another shot. I looked over my shoulder and the man was tumbling down off the tree, his raincoat catching on a little branch below the fork and tearing as he fell. Pop began to walk over to him slowly. Then he turned and yelled at me: 'Come back, you little coward! Come back here!'

The man now looked like one of those mysterious bundles of ragged and sodden clothes that you sometimes find lying under bushes in parks. Pop turned him over with his foot and stared down. I came closer, my mouth tasting horribly of the explosions from the gun – or perhaps I only smelled them. The rain was spattering on the upturned glasses and on the sticking-out yellow nose, which now looked like the beak of a dead bird. I thought that he had already gone, but he opened his eyes and looked up at me and not at Pop, and then with a kind of surprise and hurt in his voice he said, 'That was. A very. A very uncivil thing to do.'

He had told us before that he wanted to be sick and, as his body strained and his lips came forward and his face screwed up again, I thought: He's going to do it now, he's going to be sick, as he said. But it was blood that at last flooded out.

Pop turned on me in a terrible fury. 'If you hadn't let him go like that – if you hadn't chickened out—!'

I had chickened out. That was how Pop told the story and that was how I also told it. Everyone was sympathetic both to me and to Pop. The judge, summing up, spoke of 'terrible provocation to a man living under the strain of a protracted separation from those dearest to him', of 'the foolhardiness of the wretched victim's attempt to escape retribution', of a 'young boy's perfectly natural but regrettable impulse to run away at a moment of crisis' and of Pop's 'blameless past'.

At the end of it all, Pop received a sentence of one year, suspended.

Was it like that? Sometimes I can almost persuade myself it was. But then, suddenly, I still see Pop squinting at me, always at me and not at the man, as he raises that revolver under the dripping trees in the gloom of the city woodland.

A Balance of Nature

DAVID PAUL

A HOT, brilliantly clear July morning, with an absent-minded breeze just remembering now and then to send a rush and flicker of sunshine through the leaves; even London gardens, after a sweep of thundery rain, look lush, fresh and gleaming under the blue. As if echoing the blue in sound, there is a faint vibrating hum, almost like the noise in a shell, but growing; growing so that you have to watch and identify its source. Yellowish spots are shooting out down there, like dull sparks, but instead of dying they fly in widening circles, more and more every minute, intensifying and speeding up to an amazing crescendo. Mr Laxman's bees are swarming. They multiply – how many *can* there be? – until the air is dizzy with them, and they cast an immense, mad, shimmering circle of shadow over the gardens. They are streaking like shining bullets past my third-floor window.

Neighbours shoot up windows and call, and shoot down windows again. No sign of human life in Mr Laxman's garden. Unkind report has it that he is nervous, peculiarly susceptible to bee-stings, and always hides in a cupboard when his bees do this.

Meanwhile the racing circle of bees, having reached its maximum, begins to contract and darken, tilts and veers off, drawing more and more closely round a particular lilac-tree – by good luck in the Laxmans' own garden. It seems as if every bee were whirling round and down a narrowing spiral until the force of its trajectory pelts it on to the growing pile that already begins to weigh down the chosen branch. Soon there are only a few mad or lazy strays still in flight; the rest have all collected into the heavy, ominous, stirring fruit that weighs the lilac-branch down to within inches of the ground.

And now at last there is movement in Mr Laxman's garden. His immense bulk swathed from head to foot in a dark-blue gauzy veil, like some preposterous ghost-in-sunlight, or like the tragic central actor in a Noh play finally making his infinitely gradual entry on stage, Mr Laxman is advancing cautiously, skep in rubber-gloved hands, on the aberrant swarm.

A swarm of bees in July, the old rhyme comes back from some forgotten corner of childhood, *is not worth a fly*.

Bee-keeping is only one of Mr Laxman's cults. 'Caucasians they are,' he tells me, 'a very good strain, the best. Rather temperamental, though,' he adds in his floating tenor voice. 'But you must have met them often enough in your garden, without being introduced. They're not to be confused with the leaf-cutter bees – we have a lot of those around here, haven't we?'

Yes, I've seen both; in fact I had already been mystified by the perfect semi-circles cut out of the leaves of some roses and not others. And later I finally see a leaf-cutter in the act, zipping up from a rose-leaf with its semicircular slice in its jaws – as though it had fastened itself to a flying raft; a small, brown, un-bee-like bee it is, not at all to be compared with Mr Laxman's golden Caucasians.

Then in the autumn, a pretext for a genteel call, he brings round a jar of very runny honey. Does it have added sugar? It has a vague flavour of London rain-water behind the lifeless sweetness of it – brought and proffered with such deprecating ceremony. Still, his Caucasian bees have made some contribution to it.

Or have they? I cannot but think of Mr Laxman's apple-trees. Genuine they are. They are an essential part of Mr Laxman's balance of nature. They blossom for the bees and themselves, and like most apple-trees they bear apples some years; and some years they don't – thanks to a late frost, or fatigue, or temperament. And when they don't bear? I'm reminded of last autumn, a scarce year for hard fruit; though Mr Laxman's trees seem happily to have escaped. One notices the apples suddenly one shiny October morning, the sun catching their streaky reds and yellowy greens. Odd how suddenly they seem to have appeared; but that is the way one notices things – a tree covered with bloom from one day to the next, or a familiar house-front starting forth to the eye in a complete new coat of paint. The apples are certainly few, and choice, and evenly distributed – and, in fact, tied on to their twigs with little bits of thread.

'It makes a bit of a show, you know.' Mr Laxman's words – apropos of what I cannot recall – come back to me. Well, it's a principle to act on. Why not? What's the harm? His theory may be – he has a theory for everything he does – that these imported apples, hung up on home-grown trees in the smoky autumn air, will reripen, become native, acquire a sparkle, a sappiness they never had, or else lost in transit. Why not? Why not?

For all his Bacchic appearance – immense bulk, blue-veined nose, a purplish cast that comes and goes over all his skin – Mr Gerald de B. Laxman (to give him the full name he always inscribes on missives, Christmas cards, or the books he offers on loan) is an exceedingly temperate person, 'still cheating the undertaker' (one of his favourite phrases) with an abstemious diet and decoctions of various herbs – dandelion in all its forms being one of his most regular standbys: he grows them in abundance, to the annoyance and rage of his gardening neighbours. A mention of any complaint, from a headache to ulcers, will be met or followed by a murmured rigmarole of infallible natural cures.

Herbalist-by-post is in fact his main profession. He inserts small ads in a variety of remote periodicals, European, Indian, American, and particularly African. And every day his wife trundles off to the post with a trolley-basket of little parcels, sent off in reply to cash-with-orders: a modest but apparently thriving trade. His front room is his store and workshop. There are a few steel engravings of the Edwardian era on the browned-off walls – 'Wedded' and the 'The Awakening of Psyche' among others; and a large chromium-framed photograph, palely tinted, of a very flaxen blonde, smiling with shiny parted lips, and transparent blue eyes, over a coy undraped shoulder – the face is so anonymous in type it might be that of a fashion drawing, or strip-cartoon heroine. For furniture there is a battered green-topped table, two or three chairs; nothing else except boxes and boxes of herbs in the gross, and a smell of cats' messes, and a couple of cats flicking their eyes and tails at each other, in and out among the boxes.

'Must have been a bit of a lad in his day.' 'Yerse, you only have to look at him to see that!' Such is a standard local comment. But appearances, as so often, are deceiving. As Mr Laxman himself confides: 'The trouble with me, you know, is that I'm physically over-endowed. I can't touch rich food. Never could. Even a boiled egg can be too...concentrated for me. In my younger days, if I tried a mild tipple, a glass of beer would be more than I could carry!' And, even so, he looks the perfect image of Rubens' Silenus when, dressed only in what he calls his 'rompers' – a pair of very short shorts – he emerges into the sunny garden for his ration of ultra-violet rays; the rich buttery rolls of flesh are browned with years of sunbathing, and the winter sun-lamp, as he moves about, putting sticks to support the summer bedding plants, or skimming off the moss from his tiny pool with a trowel. Heavy as he is, he seems to loom and float unreal about his garden, like a balloon on tiptoe, or like that Rubens figure escaped from the canvas.

One day, forking through a pile of dead leaves and garden rubbish, I suddenly stir a tiny cry, a bubbling wail of pain and reproach – almost human, and yet unearthly in its smallness and closeness. Frozen, I can guess in a moment or two, though I have never heard that peculiar cry before, what it can only be: one of Mr Laxman's frogs. Another day, four cats are sitting in close but apparently peaceful conclave, all facing inwards; all gazing at a motionless frog in their midst. One of them solemnly advances and gives the thing a pat, to see if it is still alive and will oblige by moving again. Mr Laxman's frogs are another element in his balance of nature, though they seem unable to cope with all the rather fierce mosquitoes that breed in the pool along with them. Always a peeper and botaniser, he takes pride in having once been the nature correspondent of a local weekly, and still keeps all the cuttings; and muses on his memories of how much more nature there was in those days. A tall elm-tree, whose top is visible over the houses over the way, was once one of many, lining the path that led all the way to West End Farm. 'We used to go there barefoot as boys, to buy fresh milk.' And just a hundred yards north of us, it seems, there used to be a stately home, with an ornamental lake inhabited by huge centennial carp – all done away with in the 1920s, replaced by a small housing estate of detached villas with art deco tinted glass in the porch windows, and *comme il faut* rock gardens, and owners who lament about all the sticky stuff falling on their cars from the lime-trees that were planted with the houses. And facing one side of the estate there used to be a bank covered with scented white violets every spring. All this is just a layer of memory in an elderly gentleman's mind, inconceivable in the present that has overlaid it.

*

As for Mrs Laxman, apart from a certain unreality which she shares with him, she is the exact converse of her spouse. Where he is portentously large and pink, she is narrow, sloping and colourless: a little long in the jaw, a little battered, a little demented even – but always apologetic, grateful and gay, her head for ever tilted in a smile as she trundles along with her shopping-trolley, giving a furtive glance to see if you will speak, exchange a glad comment on the day. 'Thank you so much for stopping and speaking to me!' she astoundingly says, as she bundles on.

In their living-room opening on to the garden, Mrs L. has a piano, so rusty and untuned that neighbouring strings here and there must have got intertwined, and one key will strike two notes. Very occasionally – nearly always in light-hearted summer – she will play through her three pieces, 'The Wedding Cake Waltz', 'Moonlight on the Danube', and 'Rustle of Spring', with a sort of reckless aplomb, and then stop as suddenly as she began. It is as though time's reel, invisibly spinning, brought this moment round, with the automatic impulse to play those pieces straight through. The first time her playing was politely remarked, Mrs L. put her hands together and raised her chin, smiling as though taking a shy bow before an imaginary audience. 'As a young gel I was *devoted* to the piano! I passed all my exams right up to the eleventh grade, and then....'

But Gerald breaks in on the crisis in his wife's musical autobiography, as he invariably does on all her outpourings. Ceremonious, and even grandiloquent with all the world else, he is permanently short with her. And, like some flattened weed that has evolved a resistance to being regularly trodden underfoot, Mrs Laxman is continually abashed and yet irrepressible. On fine mornings, one hears her out in the garden, her talk winding endlessly on like an affable horn, pausing for a moment at a muttered word from her husband, then winding on again, and every now and then going off into one of her laughs.

'And just to think', she confides one day, 'that I married Gerald in the first place because he didn't know how to look after himself! He was getting on for forty years of age when his mother died and left him alone in the world. Such a baby, and he had no one at all to do for him. We were second cousins, you know, and Gerald was always a bit of an invalid. Then he went down with this terrible bout of pleurisy, and no one to nurse him but me.... Nobody else would ever have put up with all his ways, you know.'

Which is quite believable. But Mr Laxman may well believe for his part that Rose (the greyest rose in nature, surely) took advantage of him, all those years ago. A fat shy boy, an only child growing up in the shadow of a devoted widowed mother; hedged off from the world by her fondness, and taking further refuge from it in nature study, and chemistry, and photography, endlessly dabbling; and then old enough to be set in his ways and helpless without the barrier of his mother's demanding protection, once that barrier had gone. Then ill himself, ill enough, in the throes of recovery, to suggest marriage in a weak moment, all defences down. Whether so or not, he has had all the advantages since. If only Mrs Laxman sang, as well as playing those period pieces on the piano, she might well choose 'Less than the dust beneath thy chariot wheel' as her allotted ballad.

Mr Laxman's only visible chariot, though, is a bicycle that creaks and trembles under his weight as he pedals it about the quieter streets, often putting a steadying foot to the ground, and always pausing to look round in all directions at street corners. The bicycle is not so much a means to an end – though he will go as far as the seed-merchant's or the hardware stores to buy a bag of compost, a can of oil – it is more an end in itself, his form of stroll, of vague contact with the outside world. And latterly he has been using it less and less. In fact, a simple but at first mysterious substitute appears in his front garden, at right-angles to the wooden gate: a stoutish plank about a yard long and four inches across, supported on two metal uprights, about three feet from the ground. Whatever its conjectural purpose, it proves one evening to be quite simply a perch where Mr Laxman may half-sit, half-lean and take the air in front, survey the sunset, and pass the time of day, or the kind of weather it is, with neighbours as they go by, or with the few children playing about.

Mr Laxman takes a dubious view of boys. Little or big, they have the nuisance value of dogs, they trample, intrude, break windows or gates. But he has a great fondness for little girls, especially if they are flaxen-haired and blue-eyed. He gazes down at them in foolish bashful bewilderment, with a touch of incredulity that anything so small and perfect should actually be human. 'They make such beautiful photographic studies in the nude,' he once remarked to the young couple opposite, to whom he is now an object of horror and affright, 'so innocent and charming and perfect. May I photograph your little girl?' Little girls are always sure of a welcome at his house, will be given a pat on the head and a sweet, and be shown the stuffed carp (from the filled-in lake of that vanished stately home) or his pickled slow-worms, his cases of exotic butterflies, or perhaps a real live hawk-moth pupating.

One day, one such little girl, bored with playing alone in her garden sand-pit, carefully fills a blue sugar-bag with soft moist sand, and decides to take it round as a 'pretend' present for Mr Laxman. Present in hand, she is ushered through to the garden at the back where Mr Laxman sits in state, sunbathing. 'Oh, thank you!' Delighted at this reciprocation for many a candy, all unconsciously – in fact totally deceived – he plays up perfectly to the pretence. 'How very thoughtful of you, Joanna. *Brown* sugar. So much more wholesome than white. How did you know? I always use brown sugar – the pure cane: it has molasses in it, and trace elements of....' He takes out a moist lump in three fingers, puts it in his mouth and waits while it refuses to dissolve, spits and looks at his fingers, tries to wipe off a smear from his scorching chest. 'Oh, it's *sand*....' With a sudden wailing hoot, Mrs L. goes off into one of her laughs. 'Oh my goodness, did you ever. ...?' Her laugh winds on into a perfect paroxysm, stops a moment at her husband's furious 'Be quiet, will you!', pauses for breath and relief, then starts again irresistibly on a more subdued note. 'Be quiet' or a muttered 'Shut up!' is Mr Laxman's standard response to his wife. 'Oh, I knew Gerald was really unwell,' she confides one day, during one of his frequent bouts of indisposition. 'When I went into his bedroom, he asked me to sit down! It isn't like him as a rule, you know....'

'Like a perfect little doll, isn't she?' Mr Laxman's murmured approbation suggests that the fascination of little girls is that they are living dolls. They can walk, speak, change from day to day, say and do the most surprising things.

One day long ago, he took in a big doll, and in a way has been a hostage ever since. It must be twenty years or so ago, and Mr L. is now in his late sixties. Was it a tenebrous affair, a moment of daring lust, a fortyish fling? More likely it was sheer infatuated victimage. Having survived his mother's tutelage and then tied himself to a Rose he despised, he had to add one little further twist to his fate. He fell for a baby face with peroxide curls and china-blue eyes: a doll he could have for his very own! A doll encountered on one of those mild 'tipples' which had always been too much of a risk for his constitution to be indulged in very often. Miss Ireland was invited to take up residence.

Why shouldn't a gentleman with a house of his own, modest private means, and a paying little business – why shouldn't he have a *ménage à trois*; his very own doll installed on a floor upstairs, so that Mr Gerald de B. Laxman might be able to tiptoe up for chat and dalliance – a little more, a little less – a flashlight or firelight study perhaps of Miss Ireland in the semi-draped nude, fixing the photographer over a coy shoulder with her transparent eyes?

But Miss Ireland very quickly saw to it that others, too, could tiptoe upstairs; she had a preference for darker men and deeper voices, and the money they brought with them. A freelance prostitute, she had no doubt recognised a born innocent on the only occasion she had ever met one. And, thanks to that, she now had her own establishment, was indeed well set up for life, with Mr Laxman as her helpless, unpaid, and perhaps even unprotesting pimp. The doll proved to be a naughty wicked doll that must have its own way.

And now, twenty-five years or so later, Miss Ireland is a ruined doll, with a putty-coloured triangle of face, more than half of it hidden behind the dark glasses she is never seen not to be wearing; if she seems sinister, it is only because she has the quality of some non-descript, scavenging, underwater creature that lives inertly on the offal of a harbour. She has her almost nightly callers in a car, one or other of a handful of regulars who pick her up at nine or so, and bring her back towards twelve, and stay for an hour or two, or for the night; always silent as they come and go. Perhaps the relationship throughout is conducted in virtual silence – a few mutters, more drinks, and then bed. Her clients, notably a tall negro, radiate a sort of furtive gloom – resignation to a habit.

'I don't know what I shall do when Gerald goes!' Mrs Laxman's face still smiles as it tilts up and down, and she pushes her trolley-basket back and forth as though it were a baby in a pram. 'Gerald has left every thing to her, you know. Yes, the house and all its contents – everything but the piano and a few pieces of furniture of my own. Oh, no, there's nothing I can do. I wouldn't dream of it! There'll be no staying here for me. I expect I shall go back to my folks in the country.'

Cheerfully, she makes it sound like an unimaginable fate. Her folks in the country. Down what clayey lane? one wonders. But Mrs Laxman is still all thanks and apologies to life as she slopes off, pushing her trolley-basket full of little packages – elixirs of health, strength, sex or falling hair, in one herbal form or another, for the forlorn payers of cash-with-order in Utah or Nova Scotia, Seattle or Mozambique, Calcutta or Birmingham.

And nowadays Miss Ireland has taken on the reserved assurance of an owner-to-be, with a prim little nod for the neighbours which hardly expects acknowledgement, simply takes it for granted; and under her dark-blue lenses a smile like a wrinkle in stale blancmange. If she never appears in the garden, this can only be from personal choice on her part, not from any agreement. And certain edicts have gone forth – against cats, for instance. It would seem that, apart from people, and only a few of those, Miss Ireland has an increasing aversion for any form of animate nature. The cats can only be tolerated if they never encroach on her floor – a next-to-impossible injunction. So kitten production is put a stop to, and cats dispatched, until the Laxmans are left with one spayed female, Mimosa, a bundle of smoky fur and pale-green eyes, who would seem to be slightly mad, or mentally deficient – or perhaps just permanently scared at her own precarious survival. And partly from a resentment of other people's cats, which grows with his own sense of privation, partly to show a forlorn chivalrous zeal on Miss Ireland's behalf, Mr Laxman often mounts guard of an afternoon in a high armchair in what he calls his 'sanctum', where he fiddles and muses, with an eye on the window overlooking the garden – and an airgun ready to hand on the window-sill. Whenever a stray cat stalks on the dividing wall at the end of his garden, or scrambles on top of one of the oak fences at each side, it may leap in the air, scandalised at a sudden shot. If it is seen making its way among his precious dahlia plants, until it's in the clear it is spared. Mr L. is a devoted cultist of the dahlia, so far as space and his fruit-trees allow. Year after year he keeps and dries their corms, to be replanted in old oil-cans of prepared soil, or in the garden where there's room. He prefers the more demonstrative types, of soup-plate size, in dazzling yellows and reds; or else the striped harlequin sort. 'They have no scent, I agree. But they have everything else, haven't they? Mexican in origin....Curious that they should be a sort of second cousin to the potato, isn't it?' He gives a suspicion of a glance in Mrs Laxman's direction.

Meanwhile, over the years, Mrs L. has developed a terror of answering any unexpected knock at the front door. Might it be some vengeful dangerous client or crony of Miss Ireland's? Or perhaps even a police officer, a plain-clothes detective with a warrant for Gerald's arrest, for harbouring...you know who? Whatever the motive, after many unanswered knocks, there will be a strategic twitch at the window curtains, or perhaps even the flap of the letter-box will be lifted and a solitary eye peer through. But, if and when Mrs Laxman finally does open up, she will be all apologies, smiles – and relief. Perhaps poor Mrs L. feels herself an outcast in two senses: by her husband and, again, by 'respectable' society. Which might explain her profuse and amazing 'Thank you so much for stopping and speaking to me!' But, whatever her secret qualms and terrors, the neighbourhood, in its London way, takes no visible notice. No one could run a quieter business than Miss Ireland's.

Perhaps her relations with her host and hostess are almost as tacit. 'I simply won't have it, d'you hear?' She is heard one evening on her way out, giving Mrs Laxman this valediction. The words are almost completely devoid of tone, more a simple statement than a threat. But Mrs Laxman shrinks as if struck between the shoulders as she retreats towards the open front door, *still* smiling. Another time there is an exchange with Mr Laxman in the hall, again as Miss Ireland is leaving for her nightly outing, the door already standing open. His large form hovers and looms protestingly and yet timidly against the hall lamp. What they are saying is inaudible but not pleasant by the sound of it, even less so by the sound of Miss Ireland's muttered 'Fat pig' as she closes the front gate. Addressed to herself, to nobody, or to her crony waiting by the car, the words drop from that anonymous face, half-engulfed by the dark glasses, like two dead pips, like the leavings of something chewed over and spat out without relish.

It seems a long time now since Mr Laxman was seen, in his shaggy baggy brown tweed suit (he must have been one of the last men to wear bicycle-clips), manoeuvring his frail old machine about the streets, negotiating the thickening ranks of parked cars with the utmost caution. His indispositions seem to increase upon him. Even the fine-weather leanings against that curious perch by his front gate are few and far between. And poor Mrs Laxman's mind is cleft between consolation and alarm: consolation because Gerald is always so condescending and kind when illness makes him dependent; alarm for the future.

Then one day an ambulance calls, to take Mr Laxman to hospital.

And the next, true to ancient lore, superstition, or

the time of year – early July – his bees swarm once again. Evidently no one has been out to *tell them*, in accordance with the approved ritual. The whole orchestral–choreographic performance is repeated, the immense whizzing circle of bees grows denser, booming in the moist sunshine like a Beethoven crescendo; then it contracts, concentrates, settles, this time on a bush in a neighbour's garden.

For once Mrs Laxman responds to a knock at the front door with something like promptitude, – and for once with an unsmiling face. 'The bees?' Her unseeing eyes flicker in genuine bewilderment. 'Oh, the *bees*.... Mr Laxman is past caring for his bees.' She looks past her neighbour, then draws back her head, closing her eyes. 'Gerald isn't long for this world. The doctors can give *no hope*. He is sinking fast....'

The last words are intoned as if they were part of a service, or stage poetry. But any accidentally comic note is done away by her tragic accents. Mrs Laxman seems to be rehearsing a much-practised role, but one with which she totally identifies. Her bedraggled hair-do, insecurely netted, her more than usually unwashed appearance simply enhance the effect. She closes the door, her long chin just lifting from the folds of her worn green dressing-gown, with perfect timing. No play or film director could wish for a more heartfelt performance.

And so the ambulance never returns.

And within days things begin to happen in Mr Laxman's little demesne. The young crab apple-tree, shooting up long branches by his front windows, is first dealt with – by a very clumsy hired hand, no doubt. But with all its limbs lopped, chopped and bleeding it looks like a vengeance. Then the patch of soil where it grew along with two ever-recurring clumps of harlequin dahlias is methodically cemented over, to within half an inch of the tree-trunk all round – as though slow suffocation had been carefully designed for it. Next, the fruit-trees in his garden at the back are all cut to the ground. This entails so much trampling in the process, the rest of the garden is trodden to a hard clay that might as well be cement. And a junk dealer with his pony and cart calls by appointment, to take away a nondescript load of bundles and boxes.

Curiously, the perch by the front gate is still untouched. Overlooked? Not worth the bother? There it unobtrusively stays. And Mr Laxman himself, a conspicuous, odd, obstinately insistent figure, still hovers about in the memory: his appearance on Christmas morning, for instance, having knocked to deliver 'just a small greeting from my wife and self'. The air is frore and foggy, with a smear of exhaust fumes in it, and his breath seems to lave his purple face like icy steam. He must be invited in. 'This can be such a *lonely* time of year for some of us,' he breathes, almost to himself, as he moves through the hall, accepting the invitation. 'No, thanks. Thank you very much. I won't take a chair. Too much of an effort, you know, getting out of it again.' Chafing his hands, he leans and looms, taking in the whole interior, agog with curiosity stifled by politeness, noting any possible changes in the past year. 'Ah,' he tilts over a plant, with something like relief, 'I see you have a *fatshedera japonica.* Curious name, isn't it? A compound.... The plant is a hybrid, you know, between a form of ivy, *hedera*, and a Japanese plant called *fatsia.* But remarkably vigorous for a hybrid. I knew a lady hereabouts who grew one until it filled the whole of one wall of her sitting-room. Yes, the whole wall was covered....'

He leans and pauses. What to say to someone who yearns for polite converse, and who cannot risk sitting down? Yes, it is a lonely time of year. And the only questions one would like to ask are all quite impossible.

'I wondered if you'd be interested in this little thing.'

He produces something he has had in his hand all the while. 'Quite a curio, isn't it?' A single vellum page of a medieval manuscript; the verses *Magnificat anima mea* and their square musical notes are all intertwined with a trail of tiny leaves and flowers, picked out in green, violet, yellow, and gold.

'Such a pity I don't have the whole book. I don't suppose it's on *much* value in itself....Oh, do keep it awhile. I won't be wanting to read it again, just at present....'

With which ghost of a witticism he veers towards the door.

Or again, one of his last appearances comes to mind. Leaning on his perch in the May dusk, the long branches of his crab-tree still wreathed in shell-pink blossom in spite of its liberal sheddings. 'Good evening.' As his voice floats out, he lifts his face to the sky. 'I see the swifts are back.'

Sure enough, their exhilarated scream streaks the smoky luminous air just then, close overhead.

'Rain tomorrow, I'm afraid. They're flying low.'

Lost in twilit musings, and eyeing the last of the sunset over the roofs, arms folded, 'Curious,' he says, 'how one always longs for spring, and in its turn it always brings back certain longings....'

What longings? Childhood? Love?

'Such as?' I enquire, being obviously meant to be a prompter at this point.

'Oh, for the past; for the *old home*.'

The sing-song tenor lilt in his voice grows tremulous, almost caressing on those last words, the *old home*. I always understood that Mr Laxman had lived in these parts since youth, and might well qualify as the oldest local inhabitant. He must be thinking back to his earliest years. Of course there have been cloudy hints of Scottish ancestry – 'My mother's family belonged to the Macfarlane clan, you know; we have a right to wear their tartan' – and of a 'touch of the Huguenot' –

hence the 'de B.' always added with a flourish to his signature, though what the B stands for has never been elucidated.

The old hôme. What misty island, what lone shieling, what rocky Breton coast?

We stand at pause while the air darkens, the screams of the swifts recede skywards.

'I don't know what possessed me to do it.' Mr Laxman's dome of head shines dimly, and his mouth is pursed in a pout like a large bruised rosebud. 'To move house, I mean.'

Only a question can lift the weight of his ruminations.

'Where *was* your old home?'

He turns his large profile, accusingly almost, to the right, and it looks pale against the effulgent crimson of the brick wall beyond, in the still just luminous dusk.

'Number five? But you live at number seven....' Incredulity cannot quite be kept out of the voice, but it goes quite unnoticed.

'Yes. Number five,' he chimes solemnly, lifting his chin. 'You can't imagine how different it was...the orientation, the atmosphere, the whole feel of the place.' Then, after another pause, 'And, *moreover*, I didn't have that giant sycamore shading my study windows for the best half of the day.' (The sycamore has for years been a bone of contention with the old lady who lives across from his back garden, and whose own garden it more or less fills. She has always refused to have it lopped or trimmed – 'partly for the birds', as she explained to someone, 'and partly because I can't bear to look out of my window in the summer at the sight of that man, the size of him with hardly a stitch on, at his age!')

'No. I simply can't think why I did it!' With arms folded, Mr Laxman seems to confront the culprit, the former self who made that inexplicable decision.

What could have been the real motive? An impulse

to escape, shake off the influence of a departed mother, to enjoy the feel of a 'new life', with as little real change as possible?

'Of course,' he goes on resignedly, 'I approached the present occupants quite some years ago – with a view to a possible exchange. No harm in asking, was there? But of course they wouldn't consider it!'

His resignation calls for sympathetic murmurs, all the same.

'I should have liked to breathe my last there,' he continues after a moment, as if just daring to mention this. 'After all' – and his tone becomes remonstrating as well as final – 'it's the house where I was born!'

Devotion

DIANA PETRE

'Won't you change your mind and have a cup, Mother dear?'

Evie raised the silver tea-pot an inch or two from the table and, with a smile of encouragement, waited. She waited in vain. Lady Reddishaw might have been deaf and, judging by the rigidity of her pose, she might also have been stuffed.

'Just half a cup, perhaps?'

Evie knew it was useless. Mother's equilibrium had been thoroughly unsettled hours ago at luncheon by the incident with the rabbit splinter, and in trying to make things better Evie had made them worse by thoughtlessly mentioning Jane. Evie made a mental note to speak to Cook about rabbit; those little bits of bone were really dangerous. Why, an old lady of eighty-five might actually choke to death on a tiny fragment of rabbit bone. As it was, a nasty little sharp bit had somehow lodged itself underneath Mother's lower dental plate and really upset her. In trying to divert her from the indignity of having to take out her teeth at the table Evie had stupidly said the first thing that came into her head, a rare blunder after all these years.

'I do so wonder if Jane will have changed after all this time. It's been a whole year, you know, a whole year. I expect she's quite the little American by now. Her voice on the telephone had quite an American sound to it, I noticed.'

As soon as she had spoken Evie wanted to pull back

the words. With the whole of the afternoon and the early evening still to be negotiated the very mention of Jane's name was sheer folly. Evie usually managed better. Mother had always been jealous of Jane. Mother could read Evie's heart as accurately as Evie read Mother's corresponding organ, which had always pumped blood very effectively indeed, but as the seat of tenderness, if one might put it that way, ranked somewhat lower than top of the class. Nerves had made Evie careless. This morning she had woken with a headache, a most unusual occurrence for her, and although she dismissed it at once – 'No time for that sort of thing' – her eyes still felt as though they belonged to somebody else and the ache had got wedged across her forehead.

After lunch Lady Reddishaw had taken a rest on her bed. Settling her, Evie had moved a book on the bedside table a little to the left. Lady Reddishaw promptly moved it back again. Evie put the spectacles, in their case, within easy reach on top of the eiderdown. With a sweep of her hand, in imperial silence, Mother knocked them to the floor.

When the rest was over Evie got her up, took her into the drawing-room and read to her from *The Times*; then, folding the paper to a convenient size, she settled down to do the crossword puzzle aloud until it was time for tea. Mother had always been good at crosswords, but this afternoon she acted deaf and dumb except for once or twice when the withholding of her cleverness proved too much for her; then she spat out a word – the right one in each case – as though ejecting a pellet of poison.

The reason for all this pettishness was that Evie was going out for a couple of hours that evening, an event that came about increasingly seldom as Mother got older and more demanding. Jane, recently back home after a whole year in Boston living with a family, had telephoned from the country two days before.

'I'm coming up to London on Tuesday, Aunt E,' she had shouted, 'to go to the theatre. It starts at eight, but we could have an early supper together. Actually, Aunt E, I've simply got to see you. It's life and death. Could we go to a restaurant? If I come to Gran's we might be interrupted.'

Jane was Evie's god-child, one of her many nieces. On the day that she was born Evie had taken one look at the screwed-up bawling infant face and known that nothing would ever be the same again. All the other nieces and nephews were simply nieces and nephews: Jane was something else. Evie was bewitched from the start and nothing, absolutely nothing, had ever come anywhere near smudging the spell.

Evie was still trying to spin out the crossword until tea-time when the telephone rang. Getting up to answer it in the corridor, she cheerfully said, as she always did, 'I wonder who that can be!' A few minutes later she was back in the drawing-room. 'Would you believe it – Miss Birkett's gone and sprained her ankle. It seems she can't put it to the ground. So that's that; we shall have to do without her this evening.'

Miss Birkett was an acquaintance of many years who came to sit with Mother if Evie went out in the evening. It was her custom to arrive in good time for the changing of the guard, as they called it, then to help Mother get ready for bed, heat the soup which Cook, who lived out and left in the afternoon, had prepared, and to share Mother's supper with her in the bedroom.

In response to this dramatic news Mother slightly shifted in her chair; it was a movement of renewed vigour, as though a life-giving injection were just starting to have effect. 'Well, never mind,' she said quite amiably, 'it can't be helped, and no doubt the girl will be coming up to London again some time soon.'

Instead of sitting down again Evie remained

standing in the middle of the room. 'I think we'll have tea straight away,' she said smoothly, 'even though it isn't quite time for it. I shall be leaving the flat at half-past six, so we'll have to start thinking of bed at six. We don't want to be rushed at all.'

An extra stillness made itself felt in the air. Then Mother gave Evie a special and familiar look which Evie took in but managed not to meet full on. 'I know it's a disappointment, but I'm afraid you'll have to give up your evening, dear. You're surely not thinking of leaving me alone in the flat?'

'We'll talk about that over tea, if you like, Mother. I won't be gone for more than two hours. Less, really. I know it won't be as cosy for you as having Miss Birkett to talk to, but just this once we'll have to manage without her.'

Without waiting for Mother's reply Evie left the room and went into the kitchen to make the tea. When she came back, pushing the tea-trolley that Cook had left ready, a single glance at Mother told her everything: there would be no further discussion, because Mother was no longer speaking to her; nor would she touch the tea, although she always looked forward to a cup at tea-time.

Mother had never before been left alone, even for a short while, simply because Miss Birkett had never before failed them. Mother still had all her faculties and could be shielded against accidents. That evening, when Evie closed the door of the flat behind her on the dot of half-past six, she left Mother in bed, the telephone beside her, her soup in a thermos which she was quite capable of pouring without burning herself or spilling, a radio on her bedside table, her spectacles, papers and books all within easy reach.

In an Italian restaurant in Charing Cross Road, Evie settled down to wait. Jane was late. Of course. Then she came in like a hurricane, dressed in billowing clothes, all sleeves and skirts, and plopped down opposite Evie like the landing of a small parachute.

'Oh, Aunt E, you will help me, won't you?'

Evie gave a sigh of happiness. It had always been the same. Oh, Aunt E, I'm in such trouble. Aunt E, you've got to help me. Oh, Aunt E, what am I going to do? Jane never wasted time with a formal greeting. She would launch into the current tale about herself before she was well into the room. She rarely stopped talking, and often used words that Evie had to guess at; sometimes she looked as though she had gone on talking, without food or sleep, all through the night. The breath-taking egoism and steely will, the beauty of her movements, the child's unconscious and exclusive love-affair with herself would always dazzle Evie. Jane made her egocentricity seem like an art form.

The most unforgettable scene had taken place about two years ago when Jane was seventeen and still at school. In answer to the bell one morning Evie had opened the front door of the flat to find Jane standing there, her eyes painted all round in improbable colours – that day it was purple, bright pink and brown, garnished with thick false eyelashes – staring out of an otherwise ashen face. In spite of her parents' horror she had been using freaky – her word – make-up in the holidays since she was barely sixteen. Without a word she had rushed past her aunt, down the passage, into Evie's bedroom, thrown herself on to the bed, and started to howl. After a lifetime of non-participation in other people's scenes Evie had followed at a sober pace, closed the door behind her, and taken up a position at the end of the bed.

Mother's tantrums were like the crackings of a gnarled old tree on a blustery night, not to be taken seriously, just rasping to the nerves, but that morning the overflowing misery of this clown-faced child had made Evie catch her breath. She had never seen anything like it: the abandonment of the arms as they flung about; the purity of some of the notes achieved by the young wailing voice; and, above all, the voluptuous concentration.

'What is it, my lovey? Can't you tell me? Has somebody done something? There, there, you don't want to cry like that ... you'll make yourself ill.'

But Jane had seemed not to hear her. Evie never discovered what it was all about. She had not dared to touch the child. Jane did not like to be touched – at least, not by Evie; she had a way of rushing into Evie's arms and cleverly withdrawing just before encirclement ever quite took place. In a way, Evie wanted this wonderful performance on the bed never to end; ignored but very present, she had felt the thrill of the *voyeuse*. There had never been a repeat performance, even in a modified form. Evie wished that there had been.

This evening, in the restaurant, she gave her goddaughter a quick doting look-over. Jane's hair had been past her shoulders before she went away, and had hung in such a way as to mask most of her face. Now it was short, a pale cap. And the dear little face was no longer painted like a Turner sunset: except for black brushwork round the eyes the whole of Jane's face including her lips was a uniform beigey grey. She looked rather ill, but Evie knew at once that this was due to fashion rather than fact. Before Jane had taught her otherwise Evie had never looked on clothes as anything more than a part – a small part – of the routine of life. In spring and autumn she inspected her wardrobe, and Mother's, in the same way that she inspected the sheets in the linen cupboard, and when necessary, and only then, she made a replacement as identical as possible with some ageing article.

Jane had made Evie notice clothes – Jane's clothes anyway – although sometimes you could hardly call the things that Jane turned up in clothes. Once it had been no more than an Indian cotton square that she had taken off in Evie's room to show how easy it was to put on again; underneath it, like a native girl, she had had on nothing at all, not even knickers. 'Gracious me,' Evie had commented.

There was a quiet air of autocracy about Evie; she was seldom neglected by waiters. This evening, in no time, aunt and niece had studied the menu and Evie had given the order. 'Now, then,' she said, smoothing the napkin over her strong thighs, 'suppose you begin at the beginning. We'll have to watch the time. You won't want to be late.'

Jane was looking at her out of Mother's green eyes, only of course these eyes were ornamented and still young. Some strands of the front part of Jane's hair collided with her eyelashes and made her blink a few times, but she made no move to brush the wisps aside.

'I don't want to go to university in September after all, Aunt E. I tried to explain to Daddy, but he just went bananas.'

Evie had no difficulty in picturing Daddy going bananas at this news. Eighteen months ago Jane was saying, 'Daddy won't even *listen* to me. Oh, Aunt E, please talk him into it.' So Evie had offered to pay all Jane's expenses for the whole of the four years if she managed to gain a place in a university of her own choosing. Evie had made this offer in her usual practical tone of voice, and while she was making it the thought went through her mind of how surprised her brother and sister-in-law would be if they realised that, should they persist in standing in Jane's way in this matter, she, Evie, was prepared, at least in principle, to shoot them both dead. Evie herself had been surprised at her passion of purpose. Nothing on earth, she had told herself at the time, would persuade her to stand aside and allow a cruel repetition of her own story all those years ago when she was the same age as Jane.

Evie had been a big muscular girl, educated at home, with a bent for mathematics. When she had announced that she would like to go to university

Mother had murmured: 'Quoi, chérie?' Her French was not fluent, but she sometimes used this term when her full attention was elsewhere. 'Quoi, chérie?'

Evie had prudently let a few days pass and then, waiting for Mother's clear green eyes to turn her way, brought it up again. This time Mother had said: 'I really don't see how we could spare you, dear. What would the little ones do without you? What would *I* do without you?'

So Evie never went to university. She had put up no fight at all; it had never crossed her mind to do so. A little later on, for the first and last time in her life, she had got engaged to be married. She told her parents, and again Mother murmured: 'Quoi, chérie?' When Evie's fiancé was killed in an accident some weeks later the loss was fractionally easier to bear than it might have been because in a corner of her mathematical mind Evie then realised that Mother would never have let her go. It was soon after this episode that Evie knew as surely as though she were clairvoyante that she would stay with Mother. In a way, she had voluntarily given herself to Mother.

The years had passed, bringing marriage and children to all of Evie's sisters and brothers, death to her father, a steady and relentless deterioration in Mother's character – pleasure was never any nearer in her life than Tibet was – and, just when Evie was on the brink of wondering if she had mistakenly thrown away her life and not, after all, made Mother a gift of it, Jane had appeared in the world. It had been like a rescue from drowning.

Quite early on Evie had slipped into the habit of fighting Jane's battles for her; indeed, at the first sign of opposition from her parents Jane would fade away, leaving a clear field for Evie. And Evie never failed her. When an American girl invited Jane to spend the year between school and university in Boston at the family home she took for granted that Evie would back her as she always had. While the negotiations were still going on Evie wondered how the girl could possibly not know what it meant to her, Evie, to urge such a long separation, and she tried to comfort herself with the thought that a year is only twelve months. Then she'll be home again, Evie told herself.

'And what has brought about—?'

'Things have changed, Aunt E.'

Things have changed.... This phrase had been a recurring theme, like a trill in music, throughout Jane's short history. Yet what could be truer? Things, in Jane's life, *were* always changing. Unlike all the other members of her conventional family Jane had always been effortlessly modern, effortlessly in tune with present times; all the rest of the family had somehow got left behind, they were stick-in-the-muds or, as Jane would say, squares.

'You'd better tell me exactly what you have in mind.' As Evie spoke she saw the way in which Jane's face, looking more American by the minute, came alive; it also showed relief.

'Oh, I *knew* you'd understand, Aunt E. What would I do without you? It's like this. I've just gotta go back to the States. I've just *gotta* go back – it's life and death, you know? It isn't just that all my friends are there, it's – well – there's nothing *for* me here, there never has been. But over there I really dig the life – it's just great!' She looked at Evie earnestly and made a grimace of self-deprecation. 'I'm not academic, you see, Aunt E. Going to university wouldn't do anything for me. I know that now, but I didn't know it before. I thought if you could – um – well, you were going to give me an allowance, weren't you? Well, if I could have it over there instead of over here. They want me back again. Honestly. It was their idea really. And Sue – you know, my friend there – she doesn't know yet what she wants to do, either. We'd decide together, you know? I thought perhaps, after you've talked

Daddy round, if you'd write them a letter....'

Evie sat quite still. Responsive as always, she could clearly see this golden child flying off without so much as a backward glance to take up her new life among her new friends. Evie's headache had swelled up, so that Jane's slightly Americanised voice came and went in waves. Jane went on talking, making faces to illuminate a point – she did more of this than she had a year ago – and Evie sat listening to every word.

'What you're really saying is that you'd like to emigrate altogether. That's it, isn't it?'

There must have been something in Evie's face or voice that penetrated the self-absorbed castle-building, because Jane's eyes quickly went down to the tablecloth and she scratched at an invisible mark on it.

'I'd come back to see you just as often as I possibly could. Really I would.' She looked up encouragingly. 'Flights are getting cheaper and quicker all the time, you know.'

When they parted just before eight Evie said, 'I can't promise anything. We shall have to go into it all very carefully.'

'Oh!' For the first time in her life Jane gave her godmother a spontaneous hug. 'You're the most super Aunt E in the world! I knew you'd come to my rescue!'

On the pavement, alone now, Evie squared her shoulders and set off to get a bus. The first one that came was only half-full. With her strong legs she climbed up the stairs and found her favourite seat, the front one on the left, empty. She always preferred the top deck to the lower one.

Evie was about to lose her god-daughter. Jane was going for good, if not at once, then very soon. This was something that Evie's disciplined mind had never envisaged. From the early days with Mother, Evie had simply not allowed her mind to wander at will over chancy subjects – that is, subjects which might lead to emotional thoughts. Emotion was something she associated with other people, never with herself. 'I don't have time for that sort of thing,' she would say, smiling. Emotion meant trouble, and trouble was something that Evie had become expert in side-stepping or, when this was manifestly impossible, in damping down like flames. In protecting herself from the ferocity of Mother's rages, Evie had, in adolescence, resolutely turned her back on emotion.

This evening, however, emotion took hold of her as though a giant hand had grabbed her by the throat and, at the same time, something even more improbable happened: mixed up in the emotion was a suffocating rage which Evie knew to be the very twin of one of Mother's rages. Evie seemed to be seeing with somebody else's eyes, and what she saw was the robbery, by others, of her entire life. With Jane gone there would be nothing left.

Cheerfulness at any price had been Evie's lifelong philosophy. Tonight, in the bus, the hollowness of her own counsel made her mind reel into blankness. And it was then, when the impending loss of Jane seemed literally unbearable, that she was suddenly assailed by a longing so foreign to her nature and so forceful that she felt like holding on tight to her head for fear it might fly off her shoulders. She was filled with an overwhelming longing to talk to someone: to tell them about Jane and her thoughtless demands; about Mother, who would have to be coaxed out of her sulks when Evie got home; about – dear God – about every single thing that had and had not happened to Evie throughout the whole of her long life. Evie wanted to talk and talk and talk until there was nothing left in the world to say.

Nothing like this had ever come upon her before. She turned round in her seat at the front in the wild expectation that some potential listener might be sitting there only a few feet away from her, waiting for her to begin.

There were only a handful of passengers. With no especial interest they saw, turning to stare at them, a stout elderly woman with scraped-back white hair and wire-rimmed glasses, the granny glasses that were now modish on the faces of the young, and still, as they had always been, ineradicably old-fashioned on Evie's face, which, quite early in her life, had assumed the slightly pinched look of the celibate.

The bus had nearly reached her stop when the craving to talk had come upon her. In desperation she made a quick list of acquaintances – Miss Birkett with her sprained ankle? – who might allow her to talk on the telephone. But, of course, not one of them would do. Other people talked to Evie, endlessly; she had always been a good listener. Evie never talked to them.

A lifetime of self-discipline came to her aid. She now got off the bus, stood on the pavement for a few seconds and took deep sensible breaths before starting off towards home. By the time she reached her front door she was almost herself again. She put the key in the lock and went in.

'Coo-ee!'

Evie always called out to Mother as she got home, and the quality of Mother's answering 'Coo-ee!' was a valuable clue to her mood. Tonight there was silence.

'Coo-ee! Back again!' Evie cheerfully persisted.

Silence. Mother was clearly not ready to forgive. Evie went into her own bedroom, took off her coat and hung it in the cupboard. Without looking in the glass she patted her hair on both sides and then, straightening her shoulders, set off down the passage to Mother's room.

'Well, then!' she said as she went through the open door.

Sitting up in the bed, Mother was at once visible in stony immovable profile, but this sort of rejection came as no surprise to Evie; sometimes Mother took a lot of coaxing out of her icy moods. Evie went round the end of the bed and on across the room to one of the windows and straightened a curtain. Then she turned round, a bright smile on her face, and went slowly to the foot of the bed to start the lengthy and, by now, formalised process of bringing Mother round before they separated for the night. Evie had never once given up and left Mother to stew in her own acid juices; even the possibility of doing so had never crossed her mind.

'Well, then!' she said again briskly, and only then, for the first time since she came in, did she look straight at Mother.

Leaning back against the piled-up pillows, her head slightly tilted to one side, Mother's eyes were closed. She looked as though she were sleeping. But she was not asleep. Mother was dead.

Evie knew at once that Mother was dead; that the impossible had happened. The stillness was a kind of perfection in itself. She had about her an air of the utmost tranquillity, her motionless hands resting above the sheet in perfect composure. The supper-tray had not been touched; the telephone rested securely in its cradle; there had been no sudden alarm. She must have dozed off quite early on, and then, at a given moment, her heart must have simply stopped.

Without taking her eyes from Mother's face Evie reached for a straight-backed chair placed a little to the right of the bed. She drew it up close, on a line with Mother's hands, and then she sat down on it, smoothing her dress neatly over her knees.

'Now, then, Mother dear,' she said in a clear voice, 'I'm going to tell you all about it.'

And she did. Quietly, without hurrying, Evie talked. She sat upright; her straight back needed no support, and her hands on her lap lay almost as still as Mother's hands were above the sheet.

As the hours ticked by Evie went through the whole

of her long life, conscientiously leaving no milestone unexplored. Then she talked about tonight's experience on the bus when she had come face to face with the plundering of all that had been most precious in herself. There would be no more of that, she explained patiently; matters of that sort would be rearranged.

The little travelling clock on Mother's bedside table showed four o'clock and then five o'clock, but Evie never glanced at it. She talked on. One subject after another presented itself in her mind like guests at a wedding reception, and she shook hands, as it might be, with each in turn. She left Jane until the last. Ever since Evie had started talking some subterranean message had been tunnelling up from the deep recesses, seeping its way through the barriers and finally arriving in recognisable shape in the forefront of her mind. Her headache had long since gone; now she had a feeling of extraordinary well-being, and this had softened some of the lines of her face. She also felt rather drunk, and she smiled as she said, 'As soon as it can be arranged Jane is going back to America to make her life there. I shall do my best to smooth the way for her. She didn't actually ask me to go with her – well, how could she, not knowing the changed circumstances? – but I had the distinct impression that she would be happier if I were somewhere near at hand, you know, in case she needs me. So that's what I shall do, Mother dear. I now see my way clearly. I shall devote the rest of my life to Jane. I expect we'll go over together and then play it by ear, as Jane would say; but whatever happens you can be sure I won't be far away from her.'

And all the time Mother lay there, still and silent, looking, for all the world, as though at any moment she would open her eyes and murmur, 'Quoi, chérie?'

The Accompanist

V. S. PRITCHETT

IT WAS the afternoon. Joyce had been with me for nearly two hours when suddenly she leaned over me to look at my watch on the table.

'Half-past four,' she cried in a panic. 'Stop it. I shall be late,' and scrambling out of bed she started getting into her clothes in a rush. She frowned when she caught me watching her. I liked seeing her dress: her legs and arms were thin, and as she put up her arms to fasten her bra and leaned forward to pull on her tights she seemed to be playing a game of turning herself into comic triangles. She snatched her pale-blue jersey and pulled it over her head, and when her fair hair came out at the top she was saying, 'Don't forget. Half-past seven. Don't be difficult. You've got to come, William. Bertie will be upset if you don't. Ivy and Jim will be there, and Bertie wants you to tell them about Singapore.'

In a love-affair, one discovers a gift for saying things with two meanings.

'If they are going to be there, Bertie won't miss *me*,' I said. 'He used to be mad about Ivy, asked her to marry him once – you told me.'

'You are not to say that,' Joyce said fiercely as she dragged her jersey down. 'Bertie wanted to marry a lot of girls.'

So I said Yes, I would be there, and she put on her coat, which I thought was too thin for a cold day like this, and said, 'Look at the time. Hendrick will be so angry,' she said as she struggled away from my long kiss. Her skin burned and there were two red patches on her cheeks. Then she went.

It was only on her 'music days' when she was rehearsing with Hendrick that we were able to meet.

Afterwards I went to the window, hoping to see her, but I missed her. I pulled a cover over the bed, walked about and then I came across a carrier-bag on the table. Joyce had forgotten it. This was typical of her. She had more than once left things behind – earrings twice, an umbrella, once even her music. I looked into the bag and saw it contained eight small apple-pies packed in cartons. Joyce was a last-minute shopper, and they were obviously meant for the dinner we were all going to eat that evening. Well, there was nothing to be done. I could hardly take them to Bertie's and say, 'Your wife left these at my place.' Before I left at seven o'clock I ate one. It was cold and dry, but after seeing Joyce I always felt hungry.

It was a cross-London journey into the decaying district where she and Bertie lived. I had to take one bus, then wait for another. Their flat was on the ground floor of a once respectable Victorian villa. I was glad to arrive at the same time as four other guests, all of us old friends of Bertie's: André, an enormous young Belgian in a fur coat; his toy-like wife; Podge, an unmarried girl who adored Bertie and who rarely said anything; and a sharp dark political girl who worked on a review Bertie sometimes wrote for. Bertie himself came to the door wearing old-fashioned felt slippers. It was odd to see them on a young man who was even younger than we were – not yet thirty. He had a copy of *Le Monde* in his hand and he waved it in the air as he shouted, 'Well done!' to all of us in the voice of a house master at the school sports. And as we went in he was jubilant, crowing like a cockerel.

'My errant spouse', he said, 'is at this moment, I presume, toiling across the metropolis and will be here soon. You see, this is one of Joyce's music days. Hendrick's concert is coming on the week after next and he makes her rehearse the whole time, poor wretch. Of course, its awfully nice for her.'

(Bertie loved things to be 'awfully nice'.)

'He has discovered', Bertie went on proudly, 'that she is the only accompanist he can work with. It's very useful, too,' and Bertie looked over his glasses sideways at us. 'It brings in the pennies. And it gives me time to catch up on *The Times* and *Le Monde*.'

And he slapped the paper against his leg with something like passion. Then he led us into the bedroom where we were to leave our coats.

Except André, we were all poor in those days. Flats were hard to find. It had taken Bertie and Joyce a long time to find this one – they had had to make do with Bertie's old room – and to wait for Bertie's family furniture to arrive out of store from the north. As we took off our coats we felt the chill of the room and I understood Joyce's loyal but tender giggles when she spoke of it. It was, in the late-Victorian way, high and large; the mouldings on the ceiling, a thing nowadays admired, looked like a dusty wedding-cake. There was a huge marbled and empty fireplace, but – at variance with the period – brutal red tiles were jammed round it and it was like an enormous empty mouth, hungry for coal or the meals served there when the room had been the dining-room of earlier generations. In front of it, without kerb or fender, a very small electric fire – not turned on – stood like a needy orphan. Bertie was careful with money, and he and Joyce had not been able to afford to redecorate the room. One could detect small dim flowers in the grey wallpaper; in the bay window hung three sets of curtains: net for privacy, then a lighter greenish summer set, and over them heavy, once banana-coloured, curtains, faded at the folds, like the old trailing robes of a dead Edwardian lady. But it was the enormous bed that, naturally, appalled me. The bedhead was of monumental walnut, scrolled at the top, and there were legs murderous to a bare foot. Over the bed was spread a pink satiny coverlet, decorated by love-knots and edged by lace from the days of Bertie's parents, even grandparents. It suggested to me a sad Arthurian barge, a washed-out poem from some album of the Love's Garland kind. There was, of course, a dressing-table with many little shelves. One had the fear of seeing dead heroines in its mirrors and even, in the cold, seeing their breath upon the glass. I caught sight of my own head in it, looking sarcastic; I tried to improve my expression. Faded, faded – everything faded. The only human things in the room were our coats thrown on the bed – I dropped mine out of pity on what I hoped was Joyce's side of it – and the hem of one of Joyce's dresses characteristically caught by the doors of a huge wardrobe. The sight of it made me feel the misty air of the room was quivering with Joyce's tempers and her tears.

But I exaggerate. There was one more human thing: Bertie's old desk from his Oxford days against the wall near the inner door, and his long bookcase. This was packed with books on modern history, politics and economics, and here it was that Bertie would sit typing his long articles on foreign politics. We all knew – for Joyce had told us – how she would go to sleep at night to the sound of 'poor Bertie's' typewriter. She was a simple girl, but Bertie was charged by a brain that had given him a Double First at Oxford, made him the master of six or seven languages and kept him floating for years like an eternal student on scholarships, grants and endowments. In the corner stood stacks of *The Times*, *Le Monde* and other periodicals, on the floor.

'Haven't you caught up on these *yet*?' André said.

'You see, they're sometimes useful,' Bertie said. And he added with a stubborn laugh, 'Joyce, poor wretch, complains, but I tell her I don't *like* throwing things away.'

We moved into the other room.

I must say that any guilt I felt, or ought to have felt, vanished when I was with Bertie, though this evening I did feel a jolt when I saw the dining-table, which had been pushed into a far corner of the large room. Those apple-pies! Moral questions, I found, had a way of putting out their noses in small ways in these weeks. But like everyone else I felt affection for Bertie. He loved his friends and we loved him: he was our collector's piece, and in his shrewd possessive way he felt the same about us. His long nose on which the glasses never sat straight, his pinkness, his jacket stuffed with papers, pens and pencils, his habit of standing with his hands on his hips as if pretending he had a waist, his short legs apart, his feet restless with confidence like a school boy keeping goal were endearing.

His sister-in-law, the only woman to wear a long dress, and her Australian husband were standing in the room.

'And this is William,' Bertie said, admiring me. 'He's just back from Singapore, idle fellow.'

'We have just popped over from Rome,' said Ivy's husband.

Unlike Joyce, Ivy was almost a beauty, the clever businesswoman of the family. The rest of the evening she seemed to be studying me – so much so that I wondered if Joyce, in her thoughtless fashion, had been talking about us.

We sat around on a deep frayed sofa or in armchairs in which the cushions had red or green fringes so that we seemed to be sitting among dyed beards, while Bertie kept us going about people he'd met at the embassy in Brussels, about the rows on the Commission – the French delegate walking out in a huff – or a letter in *The Times* in which all the facts were wrong. The dark girl started an argument about French socialism, and Bertie stopped it by saying he had got in an afternoon's tennis while he was in Luxembourg. He was still delighted with us and swaying on his feet, keen on sending over a volley or smashing a ball over the net. This brought back to me the day he had asked Joyce to marry him. It was the only proposal of marriage I have ever heard. All of us except Ivy and her husband had been there. We had managed to get one of the public courts in the park; on the other courts players were smartly dressed in their white shorts, and we were a shabby lot. I could see Bertie, who was rolling about like a bundle in old flannels that were slipping down, sending over one of his ferocious services; I could hear him shouting 'Well done!' or 'Hard luck, partner,' to Joyce, whose mind strayed if an aeroplane flew over. I saw him sitting beside Joyce and Podge and me on the bench when the game was over, with one eye on the next game and the other reading a thick political review. It was the time of the year when the spring green is darkening with the London lead. Presently I heard him chatting to Joyce about some man, a cousin of André's who had found an 'awfully nice "niche" ' in Luxembourg. At that time Bertie had found no 'niche' and was captivated by those who had. Joyce, of course, had only a vague idea of what a 'niche' was and first of all thought he was talking about churces; but then he was on to his annual dispute with his solicitor, who wanted him to get rid of his family's furniture because storage charges were eating up the trust.

'You see,' he said, talking across Joyce and Podge to me, 'I shall want it when I get my London base.'

Joyce laughed and said, 'But you *are* in London.'

'Yes,' said Bertie, 'but not as a *base*. My argument is that I must let it stay where it is until I get married.'

André and his wife were playing and she had just skyed her ball and, waiting for his moment, André smashed it over. Joyce cried out, 'Marvellous.' She had not really been listening to Bertie. And then she turned to him and said, 'I'm sorry. I was watching André – Bertie, I meant you – you're getting married! How wonderful. I am so pleased! Who is it? Do tell us.'

Bertie gave one of his side glances at Podge and me and then said to Joyce, 'You!'

It was really like that: Joyce saying 'Don't be silly, Bertie,' and 'No, I can't. I couldn't....I....' He got hold of her hand and she pulled it away. 'Please, Bertie,' she said. She saw, we all saw, he meant it and she was angry and confused; we saw the other couple coming towards us, their game over. She felt so foolish that she picked up her racket and ran – ran out of the court.

'What's the matter with Joyce?' said André.

Bertie stood up and stared after her and began beating a leg with the review. He appealed to all of us.

'I've just asked Joyce to marry me,' he said and reported his peculiar approach.

'And she said "No",' I said with satisfaction. Love or marriage were far from my own mind; but, hearing Bertie, and seeing Podge run after Joyce in the park, I felt a pang of jealousy and loss. In two days I would be far away from my friends, sweating in a job in Singapore. Bertie heard my words and, as always when he was in a jam, he slyly dropped into French. Lightly and confidently he said, 'Souvent femme varie.'

Afterwards it struck me that Bertie's proposal was an appeal: it was the duty of all his friends to get him married. Indeed, Podge said she was afraid he was going to turn to her next. There was even an impression that he had proposed marriage to all of us; but I now see that he was a man with no notion of private life. The team spirit contained his passion and, knowing his exceptional case, he was making us all responsible as witnesses and as friends.

This passed through my mind as we all sat here in his flat, listening for the distant ticking of a taxi stopping at the end of the street. Joyce was forbidden to spend money on taxis and would come running in breathlessly saying she had had to 'wait hours' for a bus.

Conversation came to a stop. Bertie had at last run down. Suddenly Ivy said, 'Bertie, how long was this awful furniture in store?'

Bertie was not put out. He loved Ivy for calling it awful. He crossed his short, sausage-like legs and sat back with pride in which there was a flash of malice and flicked his feet up and down.

'Twenty-seven years,' he said. 'No, let me see. Mother died when I was born, father died the previous year, then my Aunt Tansy moved in for four or five years, that makes twenty-two years. Yes. Twenty-two.'

'I like it,' said Podge, defending him.

'But it's unbelievable,' said Ivy. 'It must have cost a fortune to store it.'

'That's what my guardian says,' said Bertie.

'Why didn't you make him sell it?' said André.

'I wouldn't let him,' said Bertie. 'You see, I told him it would be useful when I got married.'

We used to say that it must have been the thought of having Bertie's furniture hanging over them that had frightened off the girls he had wanted to marry. After all, a girl wants to choose.

Bertie's pink face fattened with delight at the attack.

'Joyce hates it,' he said comfortably. 'She thinks I ought to sell it.'

He was wrong: Joyce laughed at his furniture but she dreaded it.

'You'd make a fortune in Australia with furniture like this,' said Ivy's husband.

'No,' said Bertie. 'You see, it was left to me.'

He took off his glasses and exposed his naked face to us. I did not believe Joyce when she told me he had cried when she had begged him to sell it, but now I did.

If the bedroom had the pathos of an idyll, the furniture in this living-room was a hulking manufacture in which romance was martial and belligerent. Only in some lost provincial hotel, which was putting up a fight against customers, would you sometimes find oaken objects of such galumphing fantasy. There was a large *armoire* with knobs, like breasts, on its pillars and shields on the doors. Under them sprays of palm had been carved, but the top appeared to be fortified. The breast motif appeared on the lower drawers. The piece belonged to the time when cotton manufacturers liked to fancy they lived in castles. There was a sideboard which attempted the voluptuous, but oak does not flow: shields appeared on its doors. There were shields carved on two smaller tables; on the dining-table, the carved edges would be dangerous to the knuckles. Its legs might have come from the thighs of a Teutonic giantess. The fireplace itself was a battalion of fire-irons, toasting-forks, and beside it, among other things, were two brass scuttles (also with breasts), coats of arms, and legs that stood on claws. There was an atmosphere of jousting mixed with Masonic dinners and ye olde town criers.

'There ought to be a suit of armour,' said André's wife.

The only graceful object was Joyce's piano, which had belonged to her mother. It stood there, defeated.

Bertie nodded.

'You see,' he said grinning at us, 'it's my *dot*,' and gave a naughty kick with his slippers.

Father dead before he was born, mother dead, aunt dead, Bertie was trebly an orphan. He had been brought up by a childless clergyman who was headmaster of a well-known school – photos of school and Oxford groups on the mantelpiece. André and I recognised ourselves in the latter: Bertie was institutional man, his furniture was his only link with common human history.

It was not only the sacred evidence of his existence, but of the continuity of the bloodstream, the heartbeat and the inextinguishable sexual impulse of his family. He was a rarity – and our rarity, too. We were a kind of society for his protection. Joyce, who loved him, felt this; and, oddly, I did, too.

But no Joyce came, and André gave restless glances at the bottle of sherry which was now empty. Bertie saw that a distraction was needed.

'We can't wait any longer,' he said. 'Let us eat.'

He jumped up and, putting on one of his acts of pantomime, he went to the dining-table, picked up a carving-knife and fork, and, flinging his short arms wide, he pretended to sharpen the knife and then to carve an imaginary joint.

We laughed loudly and Ivy joined him.

'Come on!' she said and, pulling *Le Monde* out of his pocket, put it on the dish and said, 'Carve this.'

Bertie was hurt.

'Shame,' he said, putting the paper back in his pocket.

Fortunately the front door banged and in came Joyce, breathless, frightened, half-laughing, kissing everyone and telling us that Hendrick was giving a lesson when she got there and then would not let her go. And, of course, she had to wait for hours at a bus stop.

'Poor Bertie,' she cried and kissed him on the forehead and, shaking her hair, stared back, daring us to say anything that would upset him. She went out to the kitchen and came back to whisper to her sister.

'I've got the chops, but I must have left the pud in the taxi. Don't tell him. What shall I do?'

She looked primly at me. She had not changed her clothes, but because she looked prim (and by one of those tricks of the mind) I suddenly saw her standing naked, her long arms freckled, all bones, and standing up to her knees in the water rushing over the rocks of a mountain stream in the north where she and Bertie and I and a climbing party had camped for the night. I was naked, too, and on the bank, helping her out: while Bertie, who had refused to go into the river, was standing fully dressed and already, at seven in the morning, with a book he had opened. Bertie was unconcerned.

Yes, I thought this evening, as she looked at me; I had one of those revelations that come late to a lover. She stands with the look of a girl who has a strange shame of her bones. She pouts and looks cross as a woman does at an inquisitive child: there is a pause when she does not know what to do; and then she pushes her bones out of her mind and laughs. But that pause has bowled one over. It was because Joyce was so funny to look at that I had become serious about her.

By the time we all sat down to the meal I had advanced to the fantasy that when she laughed her collar-bones laughed. She had quickly changed into a dress that was lower in the neck, so that one saw her long throat. The food was poor; she was no cook, but André had brought wine and soon we were all shouting. Bertie was in full crackle, and Joyce was telling us about Hendrick, whom the rest of us had never met, and after dinner Bertie persuaded Joyce to go to the piano and sing one of her French songs.

'Jeune fillette,' he called. Quickly, with a flash of nervous intimacy in her glance of obedience, she sat at the piano and began: 'Jeune fillette, profitez du temps....'

Bertie rocked his head as the song came out of her long throat. The voice was small and high, and it seemed to me she carried the tune like a crystal inside her. The notes of the accompaniment seemed to come down her arms into her hands – which were really too big – and out of the fingers rather than from the piano. She sang and she played as if she did not exist.

'Her French accent', André's wife whispered, 'is perfect, not like André's awful Belgian accent,' and said so again when the song was over.

Joyce had her entrancing sensual look of having done something wrong.

'She can't speak a word of French,' said Bertie enthusiastically. 'She was eight months in Paris, staying with Ivy, and couldn't say anything except yes and no.'

'No', said André, swelling out to tell one of his long Belgian stories, 'is the important word.'

'You have Mother's voice,' Ivy said to Joyce. And to us: 'Mother's was small. And true, too – and yet she was deaf for the last twenty years of her life. You won't believe it, but Father would sing the solo in church on Sundays and Mother rehearsed him all the week perfectly, and yet she can't have heard a note. When she died Joyce had to do it. And she hated it, didn't you?'

Joyce swung round on the stool, and now we saw – what I had begun to know too well – a fit of defiance.

'I didn't hate *that*, Ivy,' she said. '*You* know what I couldn't bear! On Saturdays', Joyce blurted to us all, daring Ivy to stop her, 'after lunch before anything was cleared away he used to make me get the scissors and clip the hair out of his ears, ready for Sunday.'

'Joyce!' said Ivy very annoyed. 'You exaggerate.'

'I don't,' said Joyce. 'He used to belch and spit into the fireplace, too. He was always spitting. It was disgusting.'

We knew that the girls were the daughters of a small builder who had worked his way up and was a mixture of religion and rough habits.

'And so', said Bertie to save the situation, 'my future spouse began her *wanderjahre*, abandoned all and ran away to Paris where Ivy had established herself – and met the Baron!'

Ivy nodded gratefully.

'*Your* Baron, Joyce!' she laughed.

'Who is the Baron?' the Australian asked.

Now Joyce appealed to Ivy not to speak, but Bertie told us, mentioning he had met the Baron since those days, in Paris and Amsterdam – Bertie kept in touch with everyone he had ever met. It is painful to hear someone amiably destroy one of the inexpressible episodes in one's life, and I knew Joyce was about to suffer, for in one of our confiding afternoons she had tried to tell me. It was true that Ivy, the efficient, had started a translation bureau in Paris and the so-called Baron, a Czech exile, used to dictate long political articles to Joyce. In the long waits while he struggled to translate into English, Joyce's mind was far away.

'He always asked for Joyce,' Ivy said. 'He used to say—'

'You are not to say it!' said Joyce.

But Ivy mimicked him.

'I vant ze girl viz ze beautiful ear. One year in Paris, she knows no French, no languages – but she understands. How is zat? She does not listen to ze language. She listens to the Pause!'

'Well done!' cried Bertie.

'What the hell is the Pause?' said the Australian.

'Before he started dictating again,' I said brusquely.

Bertie looked at me sharply. I realised I had almost given Joyce away. What I think the Baron was trying to say (I told Joyce, when she, too, had asked me what he meant, for she had grown fond of him and sorry for his family, too, whom he had to leave in Prague) was that Joyce had the gift of discontinuity. She was in a dream until the voice that was dictating, or some tune, began again. She and I went on talking about this for a long time without getting any clearer about it, and I agree there was some conceit on my part in this theory: I saw myself as the tune she was waiting for.

'André,' Joyce called to hide her anger. 'Sing us your song. The awful one.'

'It's Bertie's song,' said André. 'It's his *tour de force*. Play on, Joyce – and put all the Pauses in.'

She could always take a joke from André, who looked like a mottled commissionaire. He had all the beer and Burgundy of Brussels in him, all those mussels, eels and oysters, and that venison.

Bertie's song was one of his pantomime acts to which his long nose, his eyes darting side-glances and his sudden assumption of a nasal voice gave a special lubricity. The song was a rapid cabaret-piece about a wedding night in which the bride's shoulder is bitten through, her neck twisted and her arm broken, and ends with her mother being called in and saying:

'Ci-gît la seule en France
Qui soit morte de cela.'

Bertie was devilish as Joyce vamped out the insinuating tune. We all joined in at the tops of our voices in the chorus at the end of each verse –

'Ça ne va guère, ça ne vas pas'

– even Joyce. Her little blue eyes sparkled at the words she did not understand, though André had once explained them to her. In the last chorus she glanced back at me, sending me a reckless message. I understood it. From her point of view (and Bertie's) wedding nights were an academic subject. Bertie's enjoyment of the song was odd.

'Really, Bertie!' said the dark girl who had argued with him about French socialism at dinner.

When she got up from the piano Joyce looked enviously at her sister because her Australian husband had laughed the loudest and had given Ivy a squeeze. Then as she caught my eye again her strange pout of sensual shame appeared and I felt I was slapped on the face for having thoughts in my mind that matched her own. Her look told me that I could never know how truly she loved Bertie, and feared him, too, as she would love and fear a child. And she hated me for knowing what I would never have known unless she had mumbled the tale of tears and failure in the grey room next door.

And a glum stare from Podge, Bertie's oldest friend, showed me, even more, that I was an outsider.

The song had stirred Bertie's memory, too, but of something less remote. He planted himself before me and sprang into yet another of his pantomime acts, which the sight of me excited. He put on his baby voice: 'William and I didn't have our pudding! Poor Bertie didn't have his pudding.'

Joyce's face reddened. Their everyday life, the talk of food, and money and arrangements, was irritating in my situation. I lived on my desire; they had the intimacy of eating. I must have put on a mask, for Ivy said, 'William's all right. He's got his well-fed Chinese look.'

Even Joyce had once said that about me.

'How awful of me!' Joyce cried to all of us.

I thought we were lost, but she recovered in time.

'Bertie, isn't it terrible? I left it....' (she dared not say 'in the taxi'). 'I left it at Hendrick's'

Bertie's jollity went. He looked as stubborn as stone at Ivy and Joyce. Then with one of his ingenious cackles he dropped into French, which was a sign of resolve in him.

'Tout s'arrange,' he said. 'You can pick it up on Friday when you go there for rehearsal. By the way, what was it?'

'But, Bertie,' Joyce said, 'it will be stale or covered in mould by then. Apple-tarts.'

We all saw a glitter of moisture in Bertie's eyes; it might have come from greed or the streak of miserliness in him; it might have been tears.

'We must get them back,' said Bertie.

André saved Joyce by coming out with one of his long detailed stories about a Flemish woman who kept a chicken in her refrigerator for two months after her husband left her. It became greener and greener, and when he came back with his tail between his legs she made him eat it. And he died.

André's stories parodied one's life, but this one distracted Bertie while Joyce whispered to her sister.

'He means it.'

'Tell him Hendrick ate them. He *has* probably eaten them by now. Singers are always eating.'

'That would be worse,' said Joyce.

After that André bellowed out a song about his military service and the party broke up. We went into the bedroom and picked up our coats while Joyce stood there rubbing her arms and saying, 'Bertie, did you know you had turned out the fire?'

I was trying to signal Friday, Friday, Friday to her, but she took no notice. Of course! Her sister was staying in London. How long for? What would that mean?

We all left the house. Bertie stood, legs apart, on the step, triumphant. I found myself having to get a taxi for the socialist girl.

'Where on earth are we?' she asked, looking at the black winter trees and the wet sooty bushes of the gardens in the street. 'Have you known them a long time? Do you live in London?'

'No,' I said. 'I'm on leave. I work in Singapore.'

'What was all that extraordinary talk about the Baron?' She sent up a high laugh. 'And the Pause?'

I said it was all Greek to me. I was still thinking Friday, Friday, Friday. Joyce would come or she would not come: more and more reluctant as the day drew nearer, with a weight on her ribs, listening for her tune. And, if she heard it, the bones in her legs, her arms, her fingers would wake up and she would be out of breath at my door without knowing it.

Not Like the Old Days

GILLIAN TINDALL

WHEN the black cars drew up before the semi-detached house, they were all ready and waiting. There were three cars, counting the one in front in which no one but Eric and his attendants would ride. Two others, it was felt, would be enough for the mourners. They were not a very large family, and had become dispersed with time both geographically and socially. Any friends attending the funeral would go straight to the crematorium in their own cars. After all, most people had cars these days. It wasn't like in the old days.

In the old days, all the women would have been in black, or at any rate dark grey. Eileen remembered her own mother's funeral, long ago before the war, in the little house in Deptford where they had all grown up. There had been aunts then – now forgotten dust themselves – with long black skirts, and cloaks and capes trimmed with moulting jet: lugubrious Queen Marys, they had sat in the front room all day, drinking cups of tea and talking in special black-clad voices. They would have been shocked into speechlessness to see the female descendants today. Eileen herself had not possessed a black coat for years, and was wearing her navy with a navy hat. Her sister Gladys, making a similar modern compromise, had settled for the same colour, with a blue and black patterned head-scarf. Their cousin Dorothy, the one who had had a hard life, was in what she still called her 'nigger-brown costume', which Eileen thought must be a good twenty years old; and Gladys' daughter Penny was in a reddish plaid, if you please.... Still, it was nice of her to come, Eileen told herself dully. She had cried so much over the last four days, in weariness, relief and generalised regret, that she felt completely empty, and it was almost as much of an effort to summon up decisive feelings as it was to make coherent responses to people and to think about jellies and whisky. She had also, obedient to modern custom, taken several Vallium, which she found had not improved her concentration. Fortunately Gladys and Penny were seeing to the food for afterwards, and Gladys' husband Ted was seeing to the drink. She would not, they said repeatedly, urging the tranquillisers on her, have to bother about anything.

Standing in the cramped hall pulling on her gloves (navy, too, bought yesterday) Eileen felt glad that her aunts were all dead, and many other people, too, and that it was Now and not twenty, thirty or forty years ago. She had noticed that, whereas many of her contemporaries, including her sister, idealised the past, suffering enjoyable bouts of reminiscence, she herself harboured almost the opposite of nostalgia, whatever that might be called – a degree of scorn and fear towards the past, just because it *was* the past, and over and done with. It wasn't, she considered objectively, that she had had a hard life. In certain ways (not all, of course) she had been lucky and had been spared many things. But she wouldn't wish to live it all over again, and felt impatient with those who wished they were young again or who talked about 'the good old days'. To her, long-past days, however enjoyable they had once been, were never 'good', for they exhaled too musty an odour of extinct emotions and out-of-date assumptions.

Gladys was taking her arm: it was rare that the sisters touched one another.

'You and I and George and Ruth ought to go in the

first car, Ted says; and if there's room he'll come, too. or if not he'll go in the second car with Penny and the others.'

Eileen submitted docilely, for once, to Gladys' view. It didn't matter twopence anyway, did it? They were all going to the same place. George was Eric's younger brother; he had done well in business and had a big house now in Sevenoaks, which Eileen had only once visited. Ruth (his second wife) was said to be quite a nice person, but of course she was a different sort from themselves, – you could tell that just by looking at her (today, a dove-grey dress with raincoat, shoes and handbag all to match). Eileen would never admit to being made shy by people like Ruth; after all, having married brothers, they were both just Mrs Simmonds, weren't they? But, as she had said several times to Eric, there was no point at all in trying to keep up with people who weren't your type, family or no family.

Wearily, Eileen let herself be installed in the car with Gladys on one side and George on the other. In the hearse ahead, the polished box like a cake with its creamy topping of flowers looked too small to contain an adult body – a phenomenon she had noticed at other funerals but always forgot in between. Of course Eric had lost a good deal of weight those last months, but it wasn't just that; the dead, no sooner expired, seemed to set themselves apart from the living, shrinking physically as well as psychologically, transforming themselves into alien entities at once both more and less than human. She had felt this when her parents died, when their brother Dick had been killed in the war, and when aunts and cousins and old acquaintances had died, but she had not expected to feel it so strongly and so immediately about her own husband.

She and Eric had been married for thirty-eight years. Yet she felt as estranged from the body in the box as if it had been made of another substance than her own.

She discovered to her surprise that the thought of its imminent destruction – say, in half an hour's time, or did they stock-pile bodies and burn them in batches to save fuel? – hardly touched her. '*We two shall be one flesh....*' But they never had been, not really, not like it seemed to suggest in the marriage service, and no children had grown from their union. Perhaps, she thought, that was why she didn't feel more at the mental picture of Eric's squat, plump frame being consumed with fire, appendix scar, in-growing toe-nails and all. But she had a shrewd idea that most marriages were not really the indissoluble physical union of which the prayer-book spoke. Perhaps many, many widows felt as she did, but didn't like to say so?

If she dreaded the funeral, it was for other, mundane, reasons: she was afraid of not responding to people as she ought, of not recognising some old friend of Eric's afterwards or of failing to thank the clergyman at the right moment. And did close relatives enter the chapel before everyone else or afterwards? She had meant to ask Ted, but had forgotten, and now he was sitting behind her with George's Ruth. It seemed awkward to turn round, and she felt embarrassed asking such a trivial question anyway.

Ahead, the car with its decorated box went on and on through leafy avenues, past roundabouts and housing estates. Eileen tried thinking: one day it will be me in that box. It's always been other people before, but it's coming nearer. Perhaps next time it will be me. Her depression lightened a little; she felt she had perceived something, understood in a new way what a funeral was *for*. It was a rehearsal for one's own end. Eric had always hated her to say things like that; he had called her morbid, cold-blooded, unnatural, and worse. When his mother had died and she'd said it was just as well really, wasn't it, he'd thrown the dinner she'd just cooked on the floor. But, then, Eric had gone through life with his eyes tight shut and his ears blocked, filled with generalised fear and resentment against age, time, ill-health, change, the Council, the Government, youngsters, his brother George and – intermittently – Eileen herself.

'*I am the Resurrection and the Life, saith the Lord, and he that believeth in me....*' At the sudden commencement of the chaplain's voice, Eileen raised her head. She had not, till that moment, been particularly conscious of his presence. Behind her, a few people were still creaking into pews. They shouldn't start, not really, till everyone was in, even if they *were* late, but that was cremation all over for you: just like a factory assembly-line. It probably wasn't the young chaplain's fault.

'*Man that is born of woman hath but a short time to live and is full of misery....*' Arrested in spite of herself by the force of the words, she looked at the chaplain properly for the first time.

It was Davy Lucas. Her gloved hands clutched the back of the pew in front and her heart lurched within her.

Of course, of course, she told herself as the palpitations subsided, it couldn't really be Davy. This young man could hardly have been born when Davy had used to call for Eric on firewatching nights at the house they lived in then in Lewisham and that was how it all began. But she stared and stared at him, slitting her eyes, seeing Davy Lucas' round dark head with its choirboy lick of hair over the forehead, Davy Lucas' large brown eyes and big mobile mouth with even white teeth, his slight build. Even this man's voice was rather like Davy's; they might have been to the same posh fee-paying school. Davy. After all these years.

'... *he cometh up and is cut down as a flower, he fleeth as it were a shadow and never continueth in one stay.*'

Davy had not stayed. He had, in the end, gone, quite suddenly. For three years they had known him, for half that time he and she had been lovers – and then, one day, while he and she and Eric were sitting over a scrappy meal before that night's firewatch, he had told them, just like that, that he had got himself accepted by the Army after all. Had told *them*, as a couple, so that she had to choke back her cries, her protestations. Feeling that she was indeed choking, she had got up to fetch the sweet – bottled plums, it had been, and custard made with half milk and half water as you had to then.

'But what about your asthma? I thought—'

Thought you loved me too much to leave me. You said so, once. Thought we would go on in this way for ever and ever, with you and I sharing our secret world every Monday and Thursday afternoon and you and Eric firewatching at Cruft's works every Monday and Thursday evening.

'Ah, my asthma's been better the last two years. Seems the Blitz had done it good.' She looked at him then, eager to read a secret joke in his eyes, but he wasn't looking at her. 'I've been passed Grade Three,' he said.

'They only use Grade Threes for desk jobs, don't they?' she said triumphantly. 'You'll stay in London, I expect?'

'No, actually I heard today. They're sending me to Glasgow at the end of the month.'

So he had known about his acceptance already and had not told her. The pain of it had astonished her at the time with its intensity, and now, more than thirty years later, it struck again with frightening force. Loss and betrayal swept over her like odours released from long storage, so that she felt weak and faint. In that chapel, as her husband's funeral service continued, she stood and suffered acutely, aching with new grief for a man she had hardly thought of for twenty years, eyes fixed on the stranger who was so like him.

'... *And so we commit his body to the ground, earth to earth, dust to dust, ashes to ashes....*' As he spoke, the curtains behind the coffin parted on cue as if in a cinema and the electric organ started up; the coffin itself began to move towards the gap. It was going to disappear, with its load of expensive flowers. She tried momentarily to concentrate on it, telling herself, 'I'll never see it again' – but what was a coffin anyway? A shiny box full of nothing. Instead, she found herself repeating, in a passion of love and horror, 'I'll never see Davy again. Never. Never,' as if the full meaning of the word was something which, till that moment, she had not understood.

'Well, mind you call and see us next time you come south,' Eric had said with conscious heartiness.

'Of course I will.' Davy always spoke particularly warmly towards those he did not think much of. Still not looking at her, he went on: 'I'll miss you both – and all the delicious meals Eileen's cooked for me. You've really been good to me.'

Still unable to believe the horror that was happening to her, she followed them both to the door. For an instant, as Eric was collecting coats and tin hats, Davy's eyes and hands sought hers and she realised confusedly that he, too, was suffering, but took no comfort from this. His lips framed a sentence, something about it being 'best like this'. She tried as silently to answer him, to say No, to say Wait....Half a minute later he was gone.

For weeks she felt as if she had suffered some fearful physical shock. She felt, in strict truth, as if she had been bombed out – of her own body, her own feelings. In the nights she dreamed that Davy came back to her, in many different ways and guises, but in the mornings the grief and loss were there waiting for her. She confided in no one, for that was not her way. It was all very well for the other girls at the munitions' factory where she was on the early shift to regale each other with tales of love and pain, weeping on each other's shoulders when their own incidental husbands, sweethearts or fancy men were taken away: she scorned the belittling comfort of the shared emotion, of feminine complicity. In any case, if anyone had told her she would 'get over' Davy, she would have hit them. She did not want or expect to get over him. At moments she would think consciously: 'I'll never see him again'. But she did not believe it; it was as if the word 'never', like 'infinity' or 'endless', had no meaning one could really grasp.

What happened was that, as time went by, gradually the conviction that he *would* return to her one day, though not yet, solidified into a sort of principle which she accepted but no longer examined. Only by this device could she construct some sort of sides-to-middle existence out of the shreds of her happiness. It was a repair job which, as things turned out, had lasted pretty well without further examination for the next thirty-odd years. Till now.

Only now, standing unhearing in the chapel as the service trundled to its close, did she understand. The past was not dead; it was not irrelevant or musty or contemptible but *real*, realer than the life she had lived in between. Her aunts were dead, her childhood was dead, her married life was dead, and Eric was dead and fast dwindling in size and significance, but what she had shared with Davy was not dead. It had never died; it had just lain dormant with its power intact, waiting till she should meet it again. *This* was love, the irreducible, unchangeable reality which, even when ignored, survived all deaths or distances.

In place of her anguished sense of a loss undiminished by the passage of years came a sense of joy that was undiminished also. What she and Davy had shared no one could take away. Even God, they said, could not undo the past. It and Davy were hers for ever.

Close to, shaking hands with people at the chapel door

once the ceremony was over, the chaplain did not look so like Davy. His eyes were nearer together, she decided, and his chin was not the same. He was a bad imitation of the real thing, like margarine or leatherette. It did not matter. What mattered was what he had awakened in her own mind. She thanked him automatically for the funeral service, eyes vague and deliberately unfocused.

Wreaths were laid out on a covered veranda and people were looking at them, stooping to read the cards, covertly comparing the size of one offering with another. Eileen recognised two men from the company where Eric had worked for the last twenty years before he retired, and several people from the Rotary. She smiled at them politely, veiling contempt. Old men with red necks inside their best dark suits, hanging stomachs, bald heads, bleary eyes, obtrusively white false teeth. What had they to do with her and Davy? Inside her matronly blue coat (she had never liked herself in navy anyway, she thought) she was a slim and pretty young woman in slacks and a turban, hurrying down a known alleyway in the blackout with a string bag full of vegetables in her hand and ecstasy in her heart.

Gladys, taking charge in a flustered unaccustomed way, was inviting these people back to the house. What a bore, thought Eileen, putting her gloves in her pocket. *I* don't want to talk to them. Still, all the jelly and whisky was there and must, she supposed, be consumed. She would have liked to go quietly back home alone, and change out of these clothes and lie on her bed, just remembering.

At home, a neighbour had laid all the food out on the sideboard in the lounge, where it resembled not sustenance so much as a craft display. Jellies and what she called 'shapes' were Gladys' speciality. Crystal green dressed with angelica was flanked by chocolate, by coffee and by chocolate-coffee-pink-and-plain-white blancmange in stripes like sand layers in glass from Alum Bay. Alongside, slices of candied lemon and orange hung in gelatine suspension as if in amber. The hard glossy surfaces, piped with rigid whipped cream, made it all look inedible, but at least it gave people something to talk about to get them going. Penny began plying them with plates of sandwiches (her contribution) with the abashed air of one half-apologising for their crude unpretentious reality.

Tea was made, in a large number of borrowed pots that seemed to empty too quickly. Eileen wondered when it would be considered right to start on something stronger. She and Eric always liked a drink. She knew that, if she drew Ted aside to the kitchen and asked him, he would at once press a double on her and stand there while she drank it, discreetly, like medicine. But she was sick of people like Ted and Gladys making a fuss of her. She would rather wait, politely, like a guest in her own house.

She made efforts to move about the crowded room, smiling at people and accepting sandwiches, which she then abandoned.

'... Such a nice service, I thought. Didn't you think it was a nice service, Eileen?...Oh, she didn't hear me....'

'... I thought he spoke very nicely, didn't you, Dot? Very sincere.'

'... rather *young*, but still ...'

'... Not at all like the one we got for Mother, and that only cost four pounds. 'Course, that was two years ago now.'

'...More tea?'

'... No, I won't have another ham one, thanks. Tell you what, though, is that some fish paste young Penny's got there? I wouldn't mind....'

'... No, they're with their auntie for the afternoon. I mean, they're too young....'

'... White as a sheet. So I said, "Whatever's the matter, Glad?" And she said, "That was Eileen on the phone. Eric's passed on." Quite upset, she was, it being sudden. Mind you, we were all expecting it, you might say, but it's different when it happens, isn't it?'

'... Sure? I can easily fetch some more hot water.'

'... taking it?'

'Oh, very well really, very well. But, then, she always had a lot of self-control, Eileen. She's like *her* mother in that.'

'... and we used to go for cycle rides. When the children were young. Really nice that was – lovely down that way. We used to take a picnic and that. It's all been built over now.'

'...Fifteen thousand. Yes. Of course it would be quite a bit more now.'

'...they'd forgotten all about the dog! So the postman said....'

'Thanks. I wouldn't say no....'

Finding a small oasis of space near the window, Eileen revolved in it, hands empty, trying to look contented and occupied. Presently she realised that a man was standing near her, also apparently alone. One of those fat, bald, red-faced men like all the rest of them. He said, 'I don't suppose you remember me.'

'Oh, yes, I do,' she lied easily. He was sure to be a Rotarian or someone from the bowling club or one of the regulars from the Crown; she would find out which if he went on talking. But in fact there *was* something familiar about him, particularly his voice, though he was wheezing and coughing as he spoke. She waited without interest for further enlightenment.

'Did Eric tell you he'd run into me again, then? ... Ah, I thought not. Last December, that would have been.'

'Oh, yes?' she said, computing the months. 'That would have been just before – just before his illness.'

'Yes. He did tell me actually that he was going into

hospital soon to have his – er – trouble looked at. But he didn't seem to think then that it was anything serious.' he hesitated, wheezing, then said, 'I'm very sorry, Eileen.'

'Oh,' she said, confused and puzzled that this stranger had called her by her christian name. 'Oh, well – yes. Thank you. But, after all, we all have to go sometime. That's what I tell myself.'

'Too true,' he said lugubriously, "Too true....I haven't been well myself recently.'

'Oh, I'm sorry,' she said automatically.

'No. Chronic bronchitis. At least, that's what they call it.' He coughed for a long time as if in demonstration. She recoiled from him a little. 'Asthma,' he said at last. 'They say you never really get over it, don't they?'

She said boldly, 'Where *did* you run into Eric....Run into him again, I mean?'

'It was at Charing Cross,' he said. 'I was just on my way to see my daughter. She's married now – lives in Dartford....My wife died two years ago....But perhaps you didn't know I was married?'

'I don't believe I did,' she said, feeling baffled and socially at sea. Perhaps she should have had something to eat after all – or perhaps she shouldn't have taken those Vallium pills. That was Gladys' fault.

'1945,' he said. 'My wife was from Edinburgh. When I was demobbed I worked in insurance there. But the climate never really suited me. I got transferred to the head office and we moved south when my daughter was five. We lived in Hendon. I mean, I still do.'

She thought: Why are you telling me all this? I'm not a bit interested in you. But she said, feeling that some degree of effusiveness must be called for, 'It must be lonely for you now your wife's dead.'

'Too right,' he said, coughing, 'too right.' She looked at his heavy hangdog face and tried to imagine him as a younger man, casting vaguely about in her memory for clues, but the impression he gave of age, debility and respectable undefined failure blotted out everything else. He seemed, she thought, tiresomely self-absorbed. That was the loneliness, probably.

'Actually,' he was going on doggedly, 'it's pure coincidence that I heard poor old Eric was dead. I mean, Hendon's the far side of London.'

She agreed, helplessly.

'I'll tell you how it was,' he went on determinedly. 'As I said, when I ran into Eric at Charing Cross I was going to see my daughter. Well, when I got there I told her about it – about how I'd run into an old friend from the war, and how I'd recognised him at once because he'd hardly changed a scrap, but he didn't recognise me at first. You know,' he said in a burst of desperate confidence, 'I was glad to have something interesting to tell my daughter. I mean, you try to think up things to interest them, but it isn't always easy, is it?'

'I don't know,' she said abstractedly. 'We never had any, you know.' Who? *Who?*

'Well, anyway,' he said in a rush, as if already regretting his confidence. 'I told my daughter about him. And, of course, as she lives down this way, too, she has the same local paper as you. And last week she happened to glance at the deaths column, though I'm sure she doesn't usually, and she saw about Eric. And she remembered the name from my telling her and sent the cutting to me. And that's how I came to be here.'

'So that's how,' she said faintly. Awareness was just beginning to dawn. She felt incredulous to the point of scorn, yet with every second the belief was growing.

'I bet you're surprised to see me,' he said, with a flicker of his old, debonair manner, which was followed at once by a fit of coughing.

'Oh, no,' she said at random, 'That is – for the first minute I didn't – I didn't recognise you, but now—'

Wildly ticking off points in her mind. Dark hair? He'd lost it, of course – had already been losing it actually, when she had known him; that was why he had brushed it forward in that way – and what he hadn't lost was quite grey. Eyes? Dulled and sunken. Mouth? Sunken, too. Unlike most men his age, he seemed to have rather too few teeth in his mouth instead of too many. She thought that on balance a gleaming plate would have been better. Figure? Lost. Voice?

Yes. She should have remembered his voice. Voices last, after all, when bodies have turned to flab and wasted muscle, when youth and energy and health are all spent. But his voice – though now at last she had recognised it clearly – was much altered. Between youth and age it had changed in timbre; it had been overlaid with the intonation of nearly thirty years in the company of a Scottish wife; above all, it was distorted by his continual wheezing and coughing. Asthma, indeed. His lungs must be rotting away. Perhaps that was partly why he seemed so dreary, so spent, so *old*. He couldn't be much more than sixty and yet he seemed a broken old man. Compared with him, she felt young, brisk, well organised. What on earth had brought him here this afternoon? A desire to rehearse his own imminent ending? What a cheek. What a nerve – just turning up like this. How dare he come back in this way, uninvited? Did he think that after thirty-odd years she was going to fall on his neck and beg him to come and live with her?

Her strongest desire was to turn and leave him, old, red-faced, coughing and boring as he was. He was disgusting, too, now that she looked at him more closely; not really respectable at all. His shirt wasn't clean, and there were food stains on his tie. Of course, he never had been a tidy dresser. *And always a bit of a sponger*, her mind whispered to her.

She wanted to go right away from him, away to her own room and shut out the irrelevant present. She wanted to lie on her bed with her shoes off and slip away effortlessly into the past. There, Davy Lucas would come to her, untouched by time, unchanged and unchanging. There, she would be loved for ever; he would have no faults, and all time would be one. She yearned, like a new addict, for her room, for the quilted silk bedcover beneath her stockinged feet, for peace and nothingness and ectasy. For the Resurrection and the Life that lay within herself and nowhere else at all.